More Critical Praise for Jaime Manrique

for *Like This Afternoon Forever*

"*Like This Afternoon Forever* is magnificent. On one level it is a simple and moving story of love between two poor young Colombian men, Lucas and Ignacio. Jaime Manrique tells their story in a voice that magically balances lyrical intimacy with reportorial distance; he has given us a novel that at once conveys the immediacy of art and the weight of headlines. A very special book."
—Rivka Galchen, author of *Little Labors*

"Manrique is a sophisticated rarity in contemporary letters."
—*El País* (Colombia)

"Manrique is a brilliant, agile, and supremely natural storyteller. He builds a world so deeply imagined that it seems to come from air, and so real it feels pulled directly from memory. *Like This Afternoon Forever* is both a great gay novel and a great novel, simply. It provides an intimate view of Colombia we would not have access to otherwise. This suspenseful and deeply moving story is also romantic, disturbing, sad, wise, funny, sexy, and full of truths. I will remember this book and these characters as if I knew them personally."
—Ira Sachs, award-winning filmmaker of *Little Men*

"Manrique fashions a tale of love, demystifying themes such as the amorous passion between two men, while tracing their pastoral efforts in areas of open conflict and poverty. The more you read, the more you're drawn into their story."   —*La Opinión* (Colombia)

"Jaime Manrique is a brilliant writer—compassionate, lyrical, and emotionally precise—and *Like This Afternoon Forever* is dazzling and heartbreaking, a page-turning masterpiece that kept me up for hours. I loved this book."   —Molly Antopol, author of *The UnAmericans*

for *Cervantes Street*

- Named a Latinidad List Best Book of 2012
- One of *Queerty*'s 5 Must-Reads for Fall

"Mr. Manrique structures his book around a literary mystery . . . Above

all, though, *Cervantes Street* is exciting to read ... Under Mr. Manrique's pen, the world of Renaissance Spain and the Mediterranean is made vivid, its surface crackling with sudden violence and cruelty but marked too by unexpected kindness and respites ... [T]his novel can be read as a generous salute across the centuries from one writer to another, as a sympathetic homage and recommendation ... *Cervantes Street* brings to life the real world behind the fantastic exploits of the knight of La Mancha. The comic mishaps are funnier for being based on fact. The romantic adventures are more affecting. *Cervantes Street* has sent me back to *Don Quixote*."
　　　　　　　　　　　　　　　　　　　　　—*Wall Street Journal*

"Manrique adopts a florid, epic style for his tale of sixteenth-century Spain, one with the quality of a tall tale told by a troubadour rather than written on the page. He ably captures the human qualities of the legendary writer, as well as his swashbuckling."　　　—*Publishers Weekly*

"Manrique has penned a well-written, well-researched, fast-paced narrative ... An entertaining book ... and a superb retelling of Cervantes's life."　　　　　　　　　　　　　　　　　—*Library Journal*

"Cervantes like we've never known him: the rogue, the lover, the soldier, the slave, and above all, the poet. In this novel, Jaime Manrique reminds us that the great writer was a man of flesh and blood whose eventful life seemed destined for great literature."
　　　　　　　　—Esmeralda Santiago, author of *Conquistadora*

"A sprawling vivacious big-hearted novel. Manrique is fantastically talented and this is perhaps his masterpiece."
　　　　　　　　—Junot Díaz, author of *This Is How You Lose Her*

"Author Jaime Manrique credibly fills out the unknowns in this passionate and evocative novel ... *Cervantes Street* is historical fiction at its best. Compact and intense, it is consistent with all that we know of Cervantes' life yet rich in invention. The characters are wonderfully drawn, the environments are detailed and colorful and the feeling is genuine ... *Cervantes Street* is a gripping, adventuresome novel with profound insight into the ways in which we choose our destiny."
　　　　　　　　　　　　　　　　　—*New York Journal of Books*

"Manrique's own strokes of literary genius are highlighted ... An inventive novel fortified with humor, history and graceful writing, *Cervantes Street* is a mesmerizing literary achievement."　　　　　　—*El Paso Times*

"Jaime Manrique's *Cervantes Street* is a picturesque imagining of the great Spanish master's epic life…Manrique embellishes a swashbuckling biography to offer a captivating vision of Late Renaissance Spain … By turns historical and inventive, Manrique expertly depicts a bygone era in ways that resonate with contemporary life." —*Lambda Literary*

"The novel is exciting, paced well, interesting and with a literary mystery to boot." —*Seattle Post-Intelligencer*

for *Our Lives Are the Rivers*

"Manuela has an ardent new champion, Jaime Manrique, a New York–based, Colombian-born novelist and poet, and the author of an evocative memoir about his life as a gay Latino writer, *Eminent Maricones: Arenas, Lorca, Puig, and Me*. In *Our Lives Are the Rivers*, he tells Manuela's story from the point of view of her ghost, interpolating accounts by two unusually articulate female slaves who were her childhood playmates in Quito, Ecuador. Loyal, swashbuckling Jonotás, who dresses as a man for kicks as well as for camouflage, and the more discreet Natán, who secretly questions the character of her mistress, remain her companions as she pursues her elusive lover through the continent, from battlefield to boudoir." —*New York Times Book Review*

"The love affair between Manuela Sáenz, a respectable married woman, and Simon Bolivar, Latin America's greatest hero, is brought vividly to life in Jaime Manrique's radiant new novel. Told through Manuela's voice and those of her two slaves, Natán and Jonotás, *Our Lives Are the Rivers* illuminates a momentous phase in the liberation of colonial South America." —John Ashbery, winner of the Pulitzer Prize for poetry

"A vivid portrait of a South American heroine." —*Boston Globe*

"Excels as a character study of a woman who is as emotionally explosive as the volcanoes of her native Quito, Ecuador." —*Philadelphia Inquirer*

"This juicy, deliciously involving tale, a masterful fusion of fact and fantasy, is everything we look for in historical fiction. The novel ultimately a moving evocation of compelling characters, for whom personal hunger and political destiny are one."
—Phillip Lopate, essayist, journalist, novelist

"A compelling story that melds history and biography into the context of a passionate love affair, *Our Lives Are the Rivers*, is a masterful piece of historical fiction."   —*San Francisco Chronicle*

for *Latin Moon in Manhattan*

"*Latin Moon in Manhattan* is a terrifically engaging, wondrous, and bold-hearted book."   —Lorrie Moore

"Jaime Manrique is known as the creator of an exuberant and hilarious human comedy filled with disenfranchised characters that, in general, don't want too much from life other than to experience the present at its fullest—hookers, would be poets, drug lords, and naive mothers living in a hedonistic universe ruled by sex and political corruption. They are enormously appealing."
                                    —Ilan Stavans, *Herald Tribune* (London)

"*Latin Moon in Manhattan* is an original . . . intensely human . . . picaresque and rambunctiously funny."   —*Los Angeles Times*

"If you lament the passing of legend, consider a walk with Jaime Manrique beneath the rattling rails of the elevated subway that encloses Roosevelt Avenue like a zipper—into a place called Little Colombia, Queens . . . In the mind and fiction of Mr. Manrique, it is something subtle and exquisite . . . A picaresque tale about a gay Colombian immigrant's adventures among hookers, self-made millionaires, narcotics traffickers, and elderly book mavens."
                                    —*New York Times*

"Beautifully evoked. *Latin Moon* captures well, too, many of the sights, sounds and smells of the Colombian exodus to New York."
                                    —*Washington Post Book World*

"A piece of superb satirical writing depicting the inner workings of the Colombian community . . . a welcome addition to the increasing variety of Latino writing in English."   —*Philadelphia Inquirer*

"Jaime Manrique's affectionate comedy . . . catches the East Coast Colombian Americans as deftly as Amy Tan portrays the Chinese Americans of the West. But Manrique is a giddier writer than Tan . . . a celebration . . . a Mozartian party."   —Craig Seligman, *Village Voice*

"I like Manrique's writing very much; his is an exuberant voice—both entertaining and enriching. *Latin Moon in Manhattan* captures the urban rhythms and the diversity of the Latin world of New York. This is a novel to be read."   —Oscar Hijuelos

"A novel that calmly blazes new paths. This fun, entertaining book is gentle on the reader . . . Manrique's imagination is wild and free."
                                        —Sarah Schulman, *Advocate*

for *Colombian Gold*

"*Colombian Gold* is studded with unforgettable characterizations, in a portrait of a rotten society with the bare bones of corruption poking through."   —William S. Burroughs

"With the film camera in mind, Manrique shifts scenes and spins surprising images . . . I am reminded of Malcolm Lowry's *Under the Volcano* and some of Luis Buñuel's scripts. Manrique is indebted to other novelists who have depicted the corruption of power at the highest levels—including Miguel Ángel Asturias (*El Señor Presidente*) and Gabriel García Márquez's *The Autumn of the Patriarch*."
                                        —*Washington Post*

"An excellent action novel that is at the same time a terse literary object."   —Manuel Puig

"The depiction of the left-wing movement and its issues is riveting; the inside look at the cocaine trade is fascinating; the description of the US government's war on the drug trade is mind-blowing."   —*Toronto Star*
"A dark and torrid tale about the slimy underbelly of (Colombia's) ruling elite."   —*Daily News*

"A fast-paced adventure story . . . it will keep you engrossed."
                                        —*Globe & Mail*

"[A] wild tale of . . . corruption in high places . . . inspired, but true enough that its author, Jaime Manrique, dare not return to his native country."   —*Rolling Stone*

for *Twilight at the Equator*

"That Manrique's oeuvre has become more radical, more explicit with the years is evident in his latest novel, *Twilight at the Equator*, at once prequel and sequel to *Latin Moon in Manhattan*. In it we witness Santiago's many encounters as he wanders from Spain to Colombia and finally settles in New York."   —*Herald Tribune* (London)

"*Twilight at the Equator* is a welcome addition to Jaime Manrique's considerable accomplishments, treating as it does, the complex mysteries of family and sexuality in the Americas—north and south— with dazzling cross-cultural acuity."   —Rick Moody

"Manrique writes with precision and passion, and the results are thrilling."   —Peter Cameron

"Deciding to write a novel that will kill his father, the plucky narrator of Manrique's *Twilight at the Equator* reports from a wonderfully clear-eyed center, though he roams in a series of exiles, feeling unmoored, in this provocative remembrance of early hot gay sex and learning that pleasure is never pure."   —*Village Voice*

"A powerful take on various forms of violence, suicide, political repression, sexual abuse, and the possibility of transcending them through love and art."   —*Kirkus Reviews*

Isaías Fanlo

JAIME MANRIQUE is a Colombian-born novelist, poet, essayist, and translator who writes both in English and Spanish, and whose work has been translated into fifteen languages. Among his publications in English are the novels *Colombian Gold, Latin Moon in Manhattan, Twilight at the Equator, Our Lives Are the Rivers,* and *Cervantes Street*; he has also published the memoir *Eminent Maricones: Arenas, Lorca, Puig, and Me.* His honors include Colombia's National Poetry Award, a 2007 International Latino Book Award (Best Novel, Historical Fiction), and a Guggenheim Fellowship. He is a distinguished lecturer in the Department of Modern and Classical Languages and Literatures at the City College of New York.

LIKE THIS AFTERNOON FOREVER

LIKE THIS AFTERNOON FOREVER

A NOVEL BY

JAIME MANRIQUE

Published by Akashic Books
©2019 Jaime Manrique

Paperback ISBN: 978-1-61775-715-0
Hardcover ISBN: 978-1-61775-718-1
Library of Congress Control Number: 2018912058

Kaylie Jones Books
www.kayliejonesbooks.com

Akashic Books
Brooklyn, New York, USA
Ballydehob, Co. Cork, Ireland
Twitter: @AkashicBooks
Facebook: AkashicBooks
E-mail: info@akashicbooks.com
Website: www.akashicbooks.com

Also Available from Kaylie Jones Books

Cornelius Sky by Timothy Brandoff
Starve the Vulture by Jason Carney
City Mouse by Stacey Lender
Death of a Rainmaker by Laurie Loewenstein
Unmentionables by Laurie Loewenstein
Little Beasts by Matthew McGevna
Some Go Hungry by J. Patrick Redmond
The Year of Needy Girls by Patricia A. Smith
The Love Book by Nina Solomon
The Devil's Song by Lauren Stahl
All Waiting Is Long by Barbara J. Taylor
Sing in the Morning, Cry at Night by Barbara J. Taylor
Flying Jenny by Theasa Tuohy

From Oddities/Kaylie Jones Books

Angel of the Underground by David Andreas
Foamers by Justin Kassab
Strays by Justin Kassab
We Are All Crew by Bill Landauer
The Underdog Parade by Michael Mihaley
The Kaleidoscope Sisters by Ronnie K. Stephens

for Isaías Fanlo

Like to the lark at break of day arising
From sullen earth, sings hymns at heaven's gate;
For thy sweet love remember'd such wealth brings
That then I scorn to change my state with kings.

—from "Sonnet XXIX," William Shakespeare

CHAPTER ONE
GÜICÁN
1987

LUCAS'S FAMILY LIVED ON A FARM where the days were cold and the nights so frigid that the sky frosted over with stars. The icy water that gushed from the spigot in the makeshift bathroom outside the house descended from the snowcapped mountains and it was so stinging that the members of the family only washed once a week, two or three of them at a time.

Lucas was too small to wash by himself, so he showered with his father, Gumersindo. His mother, Clemencia, and his sisters, Adela and Lercy, showered together. No one looked forward to the occasion, except Lucas who was both frightened and excited by Gumersindo's genitals. Lucas struggled to suppress the pleasure that his father's nakedness awakened in him.

One day Lucas grabbed his father's penis to soap it and Gumersindo slapped the boy's face against the lichen-covered walls. "Men don't do that!" he shouted. "Don't you ever do that again."

Lucas would never forget his father's look of disgust and his harsh tone. For the rest of his childhood his biggest terror was that he would touch his father's penis by accident.

* * *

Lucas grew up hearing about how his father was the only surviving member of a massacre that killed his entire family. Whenever he got drunk, Gumersindo would yell, "The military said that the farmers around here sympathized with the *bandoleros* and used that as an excuse to exterminate whole families! But the motherfuckers did it to steal our land! If they killed every single member of a family, there would be no one left to claim ownership of the farm." Sometimes, depending on how inebriated he was, he would start weeping as he roared, "I'm still alive because on that day I was sent to town to buy food supplies! When I got back home, I found my parents and my brothers and sisters shot in the head and hacked with machetes." He'd explode with fury, shouting, "Hacked to pieces!" Then he always added, "With their tongues sticking out from the base of their necks."

Lucas felt sorry for his father being left an orphan at the age of fourteen. He wondered how he would have managed if he had had to grow up overnight in order to save the farm, which had been in his father's family for generations. Lucas had heard many times—too many times, he thought—how Gumersindo, before he had grown a mustache, hired a married couple to help him run the farm in exchange for a place to live, food, and a share of the crops.

Lucas's father's family had planted anthuriums, sunflowers, carnations, daisies, and roses, which they sold in the local market. The soil at the top of the mountain was so fertile that in addition to the flowers, they had also cultivated the potatoes, fava beans, carrots, and roots that the indigenous people of the region ate, and sold them in Güicán's Sunday market. Gumersindo would boast to the family around the dining table: "It's a good thing I learned to read and write and have a good head for numbers. That's why we have a roof over our heads and you don't go hungry. So study; learn your arithmetic."

One rainy afternoon when Lucas and his mother were in the kitchen, sitting by the stove shelling fava beans, Clemencia reminisced about the time she met his father: "He went to Güicán for the annual festival of Corpus Christi. Gumersindo had turned eighteen and decided he should look for a wife." Then she fell quiet, as if she were unsure of stirring up a well of memories. Lucas hoped that if his mother didn't want to say more about her courtship, she would instead talk about the festival of Corpus Christi—his favorite time of the year—when the townspeople decorated the churches and plazas with flower arrangements and fruit baskets, and built bamboo arches over the street corners in the shapes of dinosaurs, cows, and horses.

"I had just turned sixteen," Clemencia continued. "Your grandparents had sent me to Güicán to study with the nuns—my parents wanted me to finish high school. We lived about twelve hours away by bus in the Llanos Orientales, where we had a plot of land and some cows. My ambition was to become a teacher in a rural school, near where we lived. The girls in the school in Güicán were allowed to go out in a large group one night during the festival, under the supervision of a nun. At the last minute Sister Rosana became indisposed. We were all disappointed—it was the only time during the school year that we could see people dancing in the streets—so the nuns took pity on us and told us we could go out unsupervised, but only if we stuck together and did not dance or talk to men.

"We didn't have money for the rides. We just walked around gawking and laughing. A group dressed in regional costumes was dancing *bambucos*. I was standing there with some girls, tapping my foot, my hips swaying, when a handsome man approached and asked me to dance. I was flattered that he had noticed me, but I told him that I wasn't allowed to dance. Then the other girls started saying, 'Oh, go ahead, Clemencia. We won't tell.' That's how I met your father. I loved dancing and he was a good dancer, and so we clicked."

Clemencia stopped shelling the beans to smooth her hair, a blush rising on her cheeks. "We danced for a while . . . When I got tired I told him I had to join my friends. But they had left already, and there I was alone with a strange man. I was attracted to him, but a little scared too. Gumersindo asked me if I wanted something to drink and I said yes. I was so thirsty I drank a bottle of beer fast without thinking. I started feeling a little tipsy. Your father said, 'Come, I'll walk you back to your school.' Somehow we ended up in a pasture outside town; I became his woman that night." Sadness came over her face. "Okay, that's enough for today. Don't look so downcast, Lucas. I'll tell you the rest some other time. We have to hurry and shell these beans or dinner is not going to be ready. You know how your father gets if his dinner isn't on the table when he gets home from the fields."

On another rainy afternoon that winter, when Lucas was helping her with the cooking, Clemencia resumed the story of his parents' courtship.

"Gumersindo started showing up at Mass on Sundays, when the other boarding students attended church with the nuns. He always sat by the front door, so I saw him as I entered and left. Eight weeks after meeting at the festival, I realized I was pregnant. I was terrified of what would happen to me when I was discovered: as soon as it was noticeable I was with child, the nuns would expel me from school. I had seen this happen to other students.

"I decided I would not go back to my parents' home in disgrace. One afternoon I snuck out of school, went into town, and began asking if anyone knew where Gumersindo lived. In a cantina a man pointed me in the direction of his farm. Gumersindo was overjoyed to see me. When I broke down in tears and revealed my condition, he told me that I didn't have to go back to my parents' home, and from that moment on we were man and wife."

When he got drunk, Gumersindo would shout, "One day I'll avenge my family! Even if it's the last thing I do!" Then he would go on a rampage through the house, breaking and smashing things and kicking the domestic animals. Clemencia raised rabbits in the kitchen. She did not eat them and treated them as her pets; she also gave them away as presents to her neighbors for their birthdays or other special occasions. Often, after Gumersindo returned home drunk, many rabbits were found dead the next morning, splattered all over the front yard. The entire family tried to become invisible at such times and quietly huddled together out of his way.

On the weekends, Gumersindo squandered his money on aguardiente and beer, and visits to the whorehouse in Güicán. After he had spent his last cent, he would stagger home in the early hours and then beat Clemencia. Over the years, the beatings became so brutal, and her bruises so noticeable, that she was ashamed to leave the farm, even to go to Mass on Sundays. Gumersindo knocked out Clemencia's front teeth, and she lost so much weight, and looked so weak, that Lucas was afraid she was going to die. On the rare occasions when a neighbor stopped by to visit, Lucas's mother would send one of the children to say that she was busy.

There was nothing the children could do to stop their father's brutal assaults. Lucas began to pray in earnest to Jesus and the Virgin to make his father stop.

One day, Gumersindo found Clemencia and Lucas in the kitchen, peeling potatoes and chatting. Gumersindo pulled Lucas from his chair and threw him against a wall. Then he started screaming at Clemencia, "That boy's going to be a faggot! He's practically a woman, all the time in the kitchen, and this will be *your* fault!" Then he turned to Lucas and bellowed, "I better not catch you here again! The kitchen is for women!"

The day after a beating, before the children had a chance to criticize their father at breakfast, Clemencia would say, "Before you judge Gumersindo, remember you didn't have to see your entire family murdered when you were children." And she'd add, "He's a good provider—you've never lacked for anything." Lucas suspected that she said those words as a kind of balm for her own bruises.

A few days after Lucas's eighth birthday, Clemencia left the farm in the morning to do some errands in town. By the end of the day, she hadn't returned. The children became worried: women traveling alone were frequently raped and murdered. That evening, as they gathered for the dinner which Lucas and his sisters had prepared, Gumersindo said, "Eat, children. I'm sure your mother's fine. She probably got delayed in town and decided to stay overnight with one of her friends." But Lucas didn't know of any friends that his mother would stay overnight with. That night, the three children snuggled together in one bed and prayed for the safety of their mother. Then they cried themselves to sleep.

The next day Gumersindo went into town to try to find out what had happened to Clemencia. He returned hours later and told the children, "I reported her missing at the police station. They promised to contact me as soon as they hear anything."

Nothing more was heard about Clemencia. It was as if she had tumbled down the mouth of an active volcano and was swallowed up in flames. A few weeks later, Gumersindo told the distressed children, "The police think your mother probably went to the Llanos to stay with her family, and that she'll return when we least expect her." He shook his head and grimaced. "Her parents will not be happy to see her when she returns home in disgrace. It won't be long before Clemencia realizes how tough it is out there. Mark my words, she'll come back home one of these days with her tail between her legs."

Lucas felt as if the sun had gone from the sky. He hated the endless drizzle and fog that swept through the house during wintertime. When the fog was impenetrable, the family walked through the house with flashlights to avoid bumping into each other or the furniture. The mist left behind by the clouds seemed to penetrate to his bones and, instead of air, Lucas felt he breathed in a cool spray. At times he imagined this made him closely related to the trout the family raised in the pond behind the house.

During those chilly months, the kitchen, where Clemencia had always kept a fire going, had been the only pleasant room in the house. His mother seemed to acquire a permanent glow from the flames of the firewood, and she had always been warm to the touch, like a toasty wool blanket.

Lucas grew even more terrified of his father's fits now that he didn't have Clemencia to hit when he was angry. Without her protective nature, life on the farm seemed fraught with dangers lurking everywhere. Instead of calling him by his name when he wanted Lucas to do something, Gumersindo would say, "Come here, *maricón*," and then bark his orders.

Every morning the children were awakened at five to feed hay to the two horses, the mule, and the donkey. Next they milked the two cows and fed them—and the sheep—hay; they fed vegetables to the rabbits, leftovers to the goats and pigs, and corn to the hens, ducks, and geese. Inside the house, they gave fresh water to the caged *mirlas* and other songbirds—which Gumersindo trapped and then sold in town—and cleaned their cages. When they were done with these chores, the three children dressed for school and had breakfast before they left the house around seven.

They walked four kilometers to the schoolhouse, on a path that spiraled all the way down to the torrid zone. They were supposed to leave together because the narrow, slippery trails skirted yawning abysses, and they had to be watchful for serpents, whose bites killed domestic animals as well as unwary locals who stepped on them.

One day Lucas decided to leave before his sisters. Since they did not tell his father, he continued to leave earlier on most days to walk alone down the mountain so he could think about his mother and not have to hide his tears.

The schoolhouse consisted of two rooms—one for children in kindergarten through the second grade, the other for those in third through fifth grade. Because Lucas was such a diligent student, and read much better than other children his age, he had been placed in the third grade. Thus he spent the school day in the same room with his sisters, who were in the two grades ahead of him. They were the first ones to notice how Lucas had changed from a studious boy to one who spent hours looking out the window. He stopped doing his homework and began to receive poor grades. But his teacher, Señorita Domínguez, did not embarrass him in front of the other students by pointing out that he was failing his subjects because she knew it was due to his mother's disappearance.

The school day was over at one in the afternoon. When they got home, Lucas's sisters quickly put together a lunch of barley soup with vegetables or rice, boiled potatoes, and string beans. Before the children ate, one of the sisters would bring lunch to Gumersindo out in the fields, where he spent most of the day taking care of the animals and the potato fields.

After lunch the children were in charge of picking the tree tomatoes, oranges, mandarins, cilantro, and onions they sold in Güicán. They also helped Gumersindo till and fertilize the soil with manure. Work stopped as the sun began to hide behind the snowcapped volcanoes in the west, their summits glowing like burning coals.

The children learned not to mention their mother's name in Gumersindo's presence. Lucas was angry that his father made no effort to try to find out where she had gone. He heard his sisters whisper that they thought their mother was staying with a relative who lived in Bogotá. His sisters became very close, united in anger at their mother for abandoning them. Sometimes Lucas thought that she had left her children because she didn't like them.

Lercy started tearing her hair out until her scalp bled. Their father bought her a wig, which he forced her to wear all the time. But the more their father lashed her with his belt for tearing her hair out, the more she did it. Sometimes she went through the house with blood on her face and streaming down her neck. After one severe beating, Lercy finally stopped pulling her hair. But one evening Lucas entered the girls' bedroom while Lercy was changing her clothes and saw her chest and stomach covered with hundreds of brown scabs. He pretended not to have seen them, but his anxiety grew worse as he worried that Lercy might leave the farm too. Instead, Lercy quit going to school.

"Suit yourself," Gumersindo said at dinnertime the night she announced her decision. "You're the one who's going to regret it later on in life." He even sounded somewhat happy that he'd have her help on the farm around the clock.

When his father went into town Lucas would wander as far as the eucalyptus grove that bordered a neighbor's property, climb a tree as high as he could go, sit on a limb, and cry until his chest began to hurt, hoping his mother would hear him and return home. After he exhausted himself from crying, Lucas would remain up in the tree, daydreaming about reuniting with his mother at the farm or far away from Güicán.

When he was alone in the house, his favorite activity was running around the dining table, picking up speed as he turned the corners. Lucas would stop when he was so dizzy he couldn't stand up. On one occasion he slipped and smashed against the glass front of the cupboard. One long shard of glass lodged under his armpit; as he pulled it out, a rivulet of blood flowed down the side of his torso. Lucas fainted.

Later, Lucas was told that Adela had come into the house with the laundry and found him unconscious in a puddle of blood. Gumersindo was off in town, so Lucas's sisters loaded him in a wheelbarrow, pushed it down to the main road, and managed to stop a bus going in the direction of Güicán, where the closest medical center was located.

The shard of glass had damaged several blood vessels and severed a tendon. Lucas had lost so much blood that, despite the transfusions, he was too weak to get out of bed for several days. The intern who worked at the medical center disinfected and dressed his wounds once a day and gave him medication for the pain.

"You need to go to Bogotá for surgery," he told Lucas. "We cannot do much more for you here."

Lucas was fed clear broth and a slice of bread twice a day, so he was happy when his sisters came to visit and brought boiled eggs, tangerines, and homemade blackberry jam. But what made him really happy was that his sisters had not forgotten him. Before they left, Adela said,

"Father told us he'll come to see you soon." Lucas didn't
dare ask if they'd had any news of their mother.

His father didn't scold him when he came to visit, but
he looked at Lucas as if he were a weakling he wanted
nothing to do with. Sister Yvonne, the older nun who ran
the infirmary, told Gumersindo that Lucas needed surgery or he was going to lose the use of his arm.

"We're too poor to send him to a hospital in Bogotá,"
his father replied. "Maybe this will teach him a lesson."

Though Lucas was horrified to think that he was going to go through the rest of his life with a crippled arm,
he did not complain. He had heard of miracles and began
to pray for one.

One afternoon when Lucas was staring out the window at the azure sky, Sister Yvonne came into the room.
She pulled a chair close to his bed. Her presence helped
to relieve his acute loneliness.

"You know, Lucas," Sister Yvonne began, "despite all
you've gone through, it's admirable that you have such
a sweet disposition. That's a gift from God, my child. I
hope you never change. When we have joy in our hearts,
we can give joy to those who suffer more than we do."

Lucas was grateful that there was someone in the
world who paid attention to him. As his wound became
infected and his arm turned red and dark blue, her kindness helped sustain him.

When his father came to visit again, he told Sister
Yvonne in Lucas's presence, "Do whatever you can for
him, Sister. I'll come to get him as soon as he's ready to go
back home. Even with a lame arm there are many things
he can do on the farm." Then he turned to Lucas and added,
"That's what happens to boys who live in the clouds."

Lucas's only consolation was the care of Sister Yvonne, who treated him with a gentleness he had only known from his mother. His arm became thinner, turned a purplish black, and Lucas could no longer lift it.

One morning while she was cleaning the wound, Sister Yvonne asked him, "Lucas, what's your favorite thing in the world?"

He didn't have to think about it. "I love animals and climbing trees, Sister."

She smiled and took his hand. Her palms were leathery but warm. "If you love animals, Lucas, you must pray to San Martín de Porres for a miracle. Do you believe in him?"

"My mother had images of him in the shrine she kept in her bedroom. He always carries a broom."

Sister Yvonne nodded. "He's always shown surrounded by a mouse, a cat, and a dog—all drinking milk from the same saucer on the floor. This scene represents his ability to communicate with animals and to create harmony among all living things."

Lucas had heard in religion class about the miracle of the mice.

"The rodents in the monastery of Santa Rosa de Lima, where San Martín lived, spoiled the grain in storage with their droppings," Sister Yvonne explained. "Traps were set to control the infestation. San Martín found a mouse caught in a trap by the tail. Instead of killing it with a broom, as he was supposed to do, San Martín told him, 'Little mouse, I'll let you go on one condition: you must talk to the other mice and make them promise that they will not come inside the monastery again to eat our grain. If you keep your end of the bargain, I'll bring food to the orchard every day so not one of you will go hungry.' San Martín kept his promise, and the mice never entered the convent again."

Lucas smiled for the first time since Clemancia had disappeared. "They say that San Martín de Porres was famous for making plants grow in times of drought," he added. "That's why farmers love him."

"He was so holy, Lucas, that he walked through locked doors and the walls of the monastery," Sister Yvonne said. "When he was asked how he did it, he replied it was God who did it, that he was just God's vessel."

Lucas asked eagerly, "What can I do, Sister, so San Martín will hear me?"

"I'll teach you the Prayer to San Martín, which you must say first thing in the morning and again right before you go to sleep at night."

Lucas began to pray with fervor to San Martín to intercede with God on his behalf. He repeated the prayer many times the first day until he fell into a hypnotic reverie. Lucas began to feel so peaceful, weightless, warmed all over, that he wondered whether he was dying.

On the third day, the sun came out earlier than usual and filled Lucas's room with brilliant light. He closed his eyes and imagined he was in God's presence. Lucas heard a door open and a lovely aroma filled the room. He pretended to be asleep. Then he thought he heard someone sobbing softly. He opened his eyes and let out a small scream of joy: his mother was there. Lucas wondered if that meant he was dead and in heaven with her. But when she rushed toward his bed and kissed his forehead and cheeks, Lucas knew she was real. It was like a miracle had happened to her: she looked strong, had put on weight, her arms were not covered with purple bruises, and her eyes were not swollen.

"I came as soon as I heard, my son. An acquaintance in Güicán wrote me at my cousin's house in Bogotá," she told him.

Lucas began to sob.

"Now, now, my angel," Clemencia said. "We must get you dressed without delay. There's a taxi waiting outside. We've got to leave Güicán before your father finds out I'm here."

As soon as the taxi left Güicán behind, Clemencia explained to Lucas that she had found a job as a live-in maid for an American couple who were Methodist missionary doctors. "They came to Colombia to work for the poor. They're good people. I told them about you before I asked their permission to come get you, and they said I could take you to the hospital where they work."

At the hospital in Bogotá, Lucas had a tendon and a vein removed from his left leg to get blood flowing properly in his damaged arm.

He remained in the hospital for almost a month. After he was discharged, he went to live in a room his mother rented for him from Ema, her widowed cousin, who owned a house in Barrio Kennedy in Bogotá. Ema worked as a saleswoman in a retail store, so she was gone all day. A gang of drug dealers had killed Alberto, her only son. Clemencia came to visit on Saturday afternoons and returned to her job on Sunday evenings.

Lucas couldn't return to school for many months. He worried he might have to repeat the third grade because of the time he had missed. The pain in his right arm was still sharp whenever he tried to lift it above his shoulder. He also limped. A government clinic in Barrio Kennedy offered physical therapy for a low fee to people with injured limbs. He walked to the clinic twice a week to do therapy for one hour. Lucas craved human contact—when the male therapist stretched his arm or leg, despite the pain, he didn't want the man to stop. The rest of the time Lucas stayed alone in the house. Clemencia would call on the phone every morning, and before he went to bed they had brief chats. But as the weeks went by, his loneliness became more acute. He missed school and not learning new things all the time; and he missed his sisters. He prayed every night that they would be reunited soon.

Ema had warned him not to let anyone in the house when she was at work. His mother forbade him to go outside to play with the other boys in the neighborhood. Every Sunday afternoon before Clemencia left the house, she would take his hands in hers and repeat the same words: "In Bogotá, there are many boys your age who are up to no good. I want you to go to school and study. It's the only way you'll have a better life than mine. Lucas, promise me you won't make friends with bad boys."

Though he longed for the company of boys his age, he promised her he would not.

Ema didn't own a TV, but she had many books about the lives of the saints. Lucas spent most of the day on a rocking chair by the front window reading those books and watching the busy street life. He kept the window closed, but he lifted a corner of the curtain so that he could peek out while remaining hidden.

Among Ema's books he found a few pamphlets about San Martín de Porres and his miracles. The more Lucas read about the saint, the more his fascination grew. He was convinced San Martín had saved his arm from amputation and had sent his mother to rescue him. His favorite stories about San Martín were those that attributed to him the gift of bilocation. San Martín was seen consoling the dying in remote villages high up in the cordilleras while he was in his cell flagellating himself to atone for our sins. There were reports of his appearances in Mexico, Africa, China, and Japan—sometimes on the same day at the same time.

A year after his accident, Lucas was finally able to return to school. His mother had been saving for his education and she enrolled him in Colegio San Bartolomé de las Casas, a private Jesuit school. Lucas studied hard, did his homework, and enjoyed the company of his classmates. The school day began with Mass, and he found himself enamored by the rituals.

During his second year, Lucas told Clemencia he wanted to be an altar boy. This decision seemed to please her. Lucas began attending spiritual retreats sponsored by the church. At these events the nuns and brothers would share stories about the Christian martyrs with the boys, and they'd watch movies the church approved of. His favorite was *Quo Vadis*.

Some nights he would lie awake in bed reliving in his mind the gory scenes of the lions attacking and killing the Christians in the Roman Colosseum, and he wept for the martyrs.

Lucas loved the fantastic stories from the Old Testament that they studied in sacred history class. But when he read the New Testament he was moved by Jesus' mira-

cles and His vow to help the poor and weak. He decided
he wanted to do his part to help relieve the pain of the
unfortunate and sick. Becoming a priest seemed the best
way to go about it, and thus the idea of helping others as
a way of life became his dream. He was never as happy
as when he was in church during Mass or when he went
to the chapel to pray on his own.

Often, after classes were over, a small group of his
schoolmates and a brother went to visit a nearby old people's home that was run by nuns. When they read the
Bible aloud to the old people, Lucas observed their wrin-
kled faces light up with smiles—even though many of
them had no front teeth left—and witnessed the sparkle
that came into their weary eyes. To see them momentarily
forget the misery of their worn-out bodies and their loneliness as he read to them filled him with joy.

Lucas also loved drawing maps: he would fantasize
about all those faraway places, and wondered if he'd ever
get to see them. While he always got high marks in geog-
raphy, history was his favorite subject with its stories of
the past infinitely more appealing and romantic than the
life he knew. In Latin, however, he was a poor student.
No matter how much time he spent studying and practicing the declensions, he barely squeaked by. And although
his mind was made up to serve God, Lucas was afraid he
was not smart enough to be a good priest.

There was something else he worried about, something that could stand in the way of him becoming a
priest. He was attracted to his neighbor Yadir, an older boy
who played soccer every day after school. Lucas would
wait all afternoon for the moment when Yadir went
by his window—wearing shorts and a sweatshirt—on

his way to the soccer field. Often, Yadir returned home bare-chested and sweaty. His legs and arms were muscular and he had a sculpted chest. Watching him walk by, Lucas relived the excitement of those showers he took with his father.

At the farm in Güicán, behind his father's back, Adela and Lercy had sometimes dressed him in girls' clothes so he could join their dress-up games. Now Lucas started wearing Ema's blouses and skirts, and covering his head with a scarf. He would sit on a rocking chair and watch Yadir go by, making sure he remained hidden.

One afernoon Yadir stopped in front of the window and said, "I've seen you watching me, dressed up like a woman. Do you want me to stick it in you?"

Lucas said nothing; he wasn't sure what Yadir meant by that.

"There's a pine grove by a stream just up the hill, behind the soccer field. I'll show you my cock. Meet me there tomorrow after school."

The following day, when they were deep among the trees, Yadir unzipped his jeans, showed Lucas his erect penis, and stood still. Lucas felt giddy; he sidled up to Yadir and tried to kiss him on his mouth.

Yadir pushed him to the ground. "That's for faggots," he sneered. "Get on your knees and open your mouth." Lucas obeyed him. Yadir shoved his cock between Lucas's parted lips. "Now suck it, faggot," he said.

From then on, on his way to the soccer field, Yadir often stopped by Lucas's house. Lucas felt an equal measure of trepidation and desire as the hour approached when Yadir would walk through the front door. They'd lie naked on his bed; Lucas would masturbate him first and then Yadir masturbated Lucas. He was aware that Yadir stroked his penis without getting excited. As soon as Lucas came, Yadir would leap from the bed and go to the bathroom to wash himself. Sometimes he would complain, "You got me dirty." Then he'd look at Lucas with disgust. Lucas knew what they were doing could get him in trouble if Ema or anyone else in the neighborhood found out. But he couldn't put a stop to their meetings because the physical contact with Yadir made him feel fully alive.

"When I take girls to the movies," Yadir told Lucas one time, "I stick my middle finger between their legs and up their asses. I want to do the same to you."

The next time they were in bed, he penetrated Lucas first with his middle finger, then with two. Lucas felt pain while Yadir's finger was inside him, but later that night he knew he wanted that pain to be inflicted again. And again. They carried on like this for many months, though Yadir never allowed Lucas to kiss him on his lips, which was what Lucas desired more than anything else.

"It's one thing to fuck a faggot," Yadir would say, "but if you kiss one, that means you're one yourself. And I'm not a homo, you understand?"

Their encounters stopped when Ema came home early from work and found Yadir in Lucas's bedroom. Yadir was dressed, and about to leave, but she must have noticed how tense Yadir and Lucas became when they saw her, and how quickly Yadir left, mumbling a rushed goodbye to her.

When Yadir had closed the front door behind him, Ema said, "I don't want that boy to visit you again when you're alone, or I'll have to tell your mother."

Lucas nodded, but avoided her eyes.

"Look," she added, "I've heard that deviates die of horrible illnesses after they have sex. That's their punishment."

The next time Yadir came to the door, Lucas opened it a crack and said, "Cousin Ema told me that if you come inside the house again, she'll go to the police and tell your family."

Yadir and Lucas never again said another word to each other. Lucas began to have nightmares that he had a terrible disease because of the things they had done. Two years passed and Lucas became frightened that his hormones had gone haywire. To diffuse his sexual feelings—which were present even when he was asleep—Lucas joined a dance group in school. The director of the group, Brother Mauricio, made learning the steps of the folkloric dances a lot of fun. Lucas noticed that his teacher favored him over the other boys. Whenever Brother Mauricio corrected one of his steps, Lucas heard muffled snickers.

Lucas had been a member of the group for several months when Brother Mauricio told Lucas that he was director of a religious community that had been founded ten years earlier. "Would you like to hear more about it?" he asked.

"Yes," Lucas said eagerly.

The next day, after classes were over, Lucas joined Brother Mauricio in his office. To hide his nervousness, Lucas sat on his open hands. Brother Mauricio pulled a chair so close that their knees almost touched. Lucas felt light-headed by the priest's proximity, but he tried hard to concentrate and listen carefully, knowing that whatever Brother Mauricio said might be of importance in his life.

On his way home, Lucas mulled over what Brother
Mauricio had told him about the community: its mission
was to listen and console people in pain, to give spiritual
guidance and assuage people's fears of death, to spread
Christ's message of humility, and to serve the poor and
the old. All that sounded admirable to Lucas. He believed
it was something he would want to do with his life.

On another afternoon, Brother Mauricio asked Lucas
to stay behind when all the other boys went home. It was
only the second time this had happened.

"Lucas, I've been watching you carefully for a while,"
he began, "and I think you have the potential to be a
good priest and could be a serious candidate to enter our
community. If you're ready to practice the vows of chastity,
obedience, and poverty, I will—with your permission, of
course—talk to your mother and explain to her that
you need to have an education that will lead to the
priesthood."

Lucas was so overcome he couldn't speak. But he
immediately worried about his continuing troubles with
Latin. He knew that mastery of the language was no longer a requirement for being a priest, now that Mass was
said in Spanish, but many of the required texts were in
Latin, and his reading comprehension was inadequate.
Though he was aware he had no particular talent that
would make him an exceptional priest, Lucas believed
that if he applied himself he would be adequately able to
console those who suffered.

"Brother Mauricio," he said with conviction, "it
would make me happy if you would talk to my mother
about my religious education."

Lucas's decision to become a priest was sealed when

he read the story of Father Jean-Baptiste-Marie Vianney, a nineteenth-century French priest. At that time, all priests were required to master Latin. Father Vianney could never learn the language well, yet he was ordained nevertheless. The bishop had said, "I will ordain him, though he lacks the brilliant quality of mind to be a learned Jesuit. We can send him to be the priest of Ars, a backwater in the Alps where the people are poor and illiterate. That will be his flock. He doesn't need a brilliant mind to do that."

Father Vianney made the long journey to Ars on a donkey. When he was in the vicinity of the village, a snowstorm hit and he wandered off the path and got lost. Half frozen, resigned to die, Father Vianney kneeled to say his last prayers. At that moment a shepherd boy appeared. The disoriented gaunt man wearing dark garments frightened the shepherd. "Don't be scared, boy," Father Vianney told him. "If you show me the way to Ars, I'll show you the way to heaven."

Soon after Father Vianney's arrival in Ars, the shepherd boy fell gravely ill. Before he died, Father Vianney baptized him, the first person to be baptized in Ars in a very long time.

Lucas loved this story and he read more about Father Vianney. He learned that the people of Ars cherished Vianney's simple but sincere sermons because his homilies related to the problems they faced in their daily lives. With the passage of years, the fame of his sermons spread throughout the region, and people began to flock to Ars on Sundays and on holy days to hear him. Toward the end of Vianney's life, famous prelates from all over Europe would come to listen to him. Though Lucas often couldn't follow the intricacies of the Jesuits' discussions of their dogma, he felt he had been shown the path to becoming a priest through Father Vianney's story.

At the end of the school year, Brother Mauricio told Lucas, "There's a good Catholic school in Facatativá, where you could go for the first three years of your pre-novitiate. Your mother can visit you often. When you finish your studies there, if you still feel you have the calling, you can go on to the seminary and become ordained."

As his dream to become a priest seemed more within reach, Lucas was both excited and afraid. He knew that if he continued on this path, soon there would be no turning back.

Perhaps sensing Lucas's doubts, Brother Mauricio told him, "It's clear to me you have a gift for consoling those in pain, and for spreading Jesus' message of humility and service. Lucas, do you think you're ready to devote your life to Jesus?"

"I'm ready, Father," he said, without hesitation. At that moment, he prayed that if he became a priest his feelings for men would go away.

"Now all we need to do," Brother Mauricio said, "is convince your mother to send you to Colegio San José in Facatativá."

When Lucas told his mother the news, Clemencia, instead of being upset, said, "Nothing would make me happier than to have my son dedicated to the service of God." She embraced him tightly and did not say another word about the subject.

C

HAPTER TWO
FACATATIVÁ
1992

IT WAS AT COLEGIO SAN JOSÉ in Facatativá that Lucas met Ignacio Gutiérrez. Ignacio had arrived at the school just days before the beginning of classes. They spoke for the first time in the courtyard, during the free hour after classes had ended. Ignacio was standing by himself leaning against a wall, rhythmically moving a foot back and forth on the grassy ground. He stood out from the other seminarians because of his copper-colored skin. From the moment Lucas saw Ignacio's shining black eyes, he was mesmerized. Lucas approached him.

"I'm Ignacio. I'm a Barí," the young man blurted out. Then almost boastfully, he added, "I have no white blood in me." Ignacio spoke with the peasant accent from a part of Colombia Lucas knew little about.

Lucas had heard of the Barí people before, but that was all—so he didn't know how to reply. Ignacio had thick, gleaming obsidian hair and long, abundant eyelashes the same color. *He looks like a panther*, Lucas thought, wanting to touch the young man's hair. He shook his head to break off Ignacio's transfixing spell. "My name is Lucas," he finally managed to say.

"I don't like it here," Ignacio muttered. "Do you?"

Lucas didn't answer his question for fear of not saying the right thing and alienating this fascinating new student. He wanted to be his friend more than he had wanted anything in a long time.

Ignacio continued, "I'm here because my first two brothers were stillborn, so my parents pledged to the Virgin of Chiquinquirá that the firstborn son who survived childbirth would be offered to the church. Even before I was born, my parents referred to me as 'the priest.'"

The angry tone in which Ignacio said these words made it sound as if he had been cursed. Lucas expected him to spit at the ground. The other students did not speak with such vehemence or honesty. Every word that came out of Ignacio's mouth was like a blow aimed right at Lucas.

A part of Lucas was repelled, but another part was drawn to Ignacio's magnetism. He represented temptation—everything that Lucas had been afraid of all his life. He sensed he had met someone who was going to be an important figure during his time in Colegio San José. Lucas felt pity for Ignacio because it was obvious he was unhappy. He didn't seem interested in casual chat. The other students, with their mundane concerns, suddenly became uninteresting to Lucas.

"After I was born," Ignacio told Lucas the second time they talked, "came five sisters. I was the only son. I wasn't one of those boys who like going to church and hanging out around priests. But when my parents told me that I should prepare myself to come here, I didn't argue with them." He seemed greatly relieved to say these things to Lucas, as if for the first time he had someone he could talk to openly about his feelings for the priesthood. Lucas felt awkward hearing what he thought sounded like a secret. He wondered if this was what priests experienced when they heard confession.

Ignacio rebuffed other boys when they approached him. Lucas quickly realized that he would be Ignacio's only friend during their years at Colegio San José. The prospect thrilled and disturbed him—he felt it was both an honor and a burden.

After they had chatted a few times, Lucas was gripped by an overpowering need to be with Ignacio. At mealtimes Lucas sat across from him. During recess, they walked by themselves in the yard. They never participated in team sports. Happiness for Lucas was being by Ignacio's side, even when his friend was quiet, brooding. Lucas began to feel that it was the two of them against the world.

Their teachers discouraged this kind of intimacy; the other boys were wary of the stigma attached to two boys who were always seen together. It was as if Lucas wanted to fuse into one person with Ignacio and disappear into him. With Ignacio constantly in his thoughts, Lucas didn't feel lonely anymore. For the first time in his life, he felt that he could face any situation—no matter how challenging—as long as Ignacio was by his side.

Lucas knew that their intimate friendship could get in the way of his being ordained, but the physical need to be near this angry boy was stronger than his fears. When he was talking with Ignacio he felt so happy that he told himself he didn't care about the consequences. Had he perhaps found what he had heard people call a soul mate?

Ignacio always studied his lessons, did his homework, and got the highest marks in the quizzes and exams, yet the teachers didn't hide their dislike of him because of his intellectual arrogance. In religion class, he constantly questioned the meaning of the Scriptures. One day they were talking about Judas's betrayal of Jesus. Brother Mariano presented Judas as a despicable creature and the other boys nodded in agreement.

Ignacio raised his hand. "Brother Mariano, with all due respect," he began, as the classroom became eerily quiet in anticipation of a heated argument, "why is Judas Iscariot considered such a vile creature, when it was written that one of the disciples would betray Jesus?"

"That's right," Father Mariano replied curtly. "But when Judas was tempted by Satan, he should have exercised his free will and resisted temptation—that's what separates man from beasts."

Instead of backing down, Ignacio became more intense: "But if it was written that one of the disciples was going to betray Jesus, how could any of them have exercised his free will? One apostle *had* to be sacrificed to agree with the Scriptures. Is that fair? Isn't God supposed to be all wisdom?"

Murmurs and titters broke out in the classroom. Lucas became agitated when he sensed that Ignacio was getting too reckless. Brother Mariano slammed his open palm on the desk and raised his voice, his face red: "More illustrious and enlightened minds than yours, Gutiérrez, have argued this point for many centuries. If they haven't come up with a more satisfactory answer, I doubt that you will."

Ignacio was unwilling to let the subject go. Lucas knew that when Ignacio was defending his ideas, he was like a dog ready to kill for a fleshy bone. "But Brother

Mariano, how can I believe in something that makes no sense to me?"

Brother Mariano got up from his desk and walked toward Ignacio, glaring at him. His fists were clenched and the veins in his neck pulsed. He looked like he might punch the student. "That's where faith comes in, Gutiérrez. Faith! And nobody can be a priest without having faith." He closed his eyes, took a deep breath, and went back to stand behind his desk. "I warn you, Gutiérrez, if you persist in disrupting this class, I will send you to see Father Superior. He doesn't look kindly on insolent boys." In an ominous tone, he added, "It especially behooves certain boys here to behave well." Lucas knew that meant that scholarship students—like Ignacio and himself—were expected to be meek.

The other students began to squirm, and just as Ignacio was about to respond, the bell rang and class was dismissed. That day Ignacio made many enemies, but he seemed not to care about it.

As Ignacio's only friend, Lucas knew that he was in danger of being singled out as a troublemaker, or a *homo*. But he was more worried about his feelings for Ignacio. He tried to convince himself that what he felt for him was brotherly love, and that it was Jesus who had brought them together. He prayed to Jesus to intervene and to remove from his mind all overwhelming carnal desires.

Lucas was sure his religious fervor was genuine and his faith in God was unshakable. Unlike Ignacio, he didn't feel the need to question God's acts. He also understood that his deepest relationship should not be with Ignacio but with Jesus. He desperately wanted to embrace what it meant to be a good Catholic worthy of the priesthood. Besides, the students at Colegio San José had been warned about two boys in the class before theirs who had been expelled because of their unnaturally close friendship. Everyone knew what that meant.

Though he had been taught that masturbation would lead to blindness and then madness, Lucas could not stop himself. Despite the painful experience he'd had in Bogotá with Yadir, he still longed to be touched by a man. He could not stop himself from having fantasies about pleasuring Ignacio. As he played with himself, he imagined lying naked with Ignacio, kissing and stroking him, and then waking up from a nap in each other's arms. Or he fantasized about sneaking over to Ignacio's bed in the middle of the night and taking his penis in his mouth, while Ignacio pretended to sleep.

Going to confession became agony for Lucas: he knew that he could not mention any of these thoughts to his Father confessor. He had heard other boys say that it was better to deny having masturbated, even if it meant they were committing a mortal sin.

Lucas prayed that he would be strong enough to overcome his feelings for Ignacio, yet how could he when Ignacio sought his company to the exclusion of the other boys? Did that mean he reciprocated Lucas's feelings? Or did he seek Lucas's company because he could not trust the other students? Lucas was proud he had been chosen as the best friend of the most intelligent boy in the school, yet he lived in terror that he'd say something that betrayed his feelings for Ignacio and expose himself as homosexual. Lucas made sure he didn't touch him in any way, just as he had avoided touching his father's penis, even by accident. Still, he could not stop wondering how Ignacio would react if he made a sudden move and embraced him with lust, or kissed him on his lips. Would he hit him? Reject him? Denounce him to the teachers? Would he lose his friendship forever?

Lucas's worst fear was that if his teachers had proof that he liked boys, he would be expelled. He could not bear the thought of disappointing his mother, who still grieved intensely that she had had to leave Adela and Lercy behind so she and Lucas could escape Gumersindo's tyranny. Lucas believed that loving Ignacio was a betrayal of the love he owed Jesus Christ. He felt the shame of betraying God. Sex outside of marriage was a sin, they were told, over and over again. And sex between men was an abomination. Lucas was tortured by the real possibility that his shameful desires would lead to his ruin.

He could not concentrate during classes and became so distracted that he began to turn in his homework late. As a partial scholarship student, he was expected to excel academically. Scholarship students were constantly reminded that there were many other boys who were ready to take their places at Colegio San José if their academic performance was mediocre.

Lucas had also become increasingly aware of the special bond some priests had with the boys they fancied. There was intense competition among the students to become a "favorite." No stigma was attached to being a priest's favorite boy. Lucas was relieved that no priest had shown an interest in him, but because he and Ignacio spent so much time together, he was the focus of malicious gossip. Some teachers gave them disapproving looks when they saw them together; and the sneers of students followed them as they walked through the long chilly corridors of Colegio San José. The effeminate boys were often bullied, but no one dared to torment him or Ignacio because Ignacio, though smallish and lean, had the powerful shoulders of a bull calf; when he gave the students glances of displeasure, he looked menacing and ready to disembowel them.

Still, Lucas grew concerned when the sneers became accusatory looks. His concern turned into alarm when he found notes under his pillow, as well as inside his desk, that said *Faggot!* and *Cocksucker!* But to complain to one of the teachers would have been in itself a kind of admission. Even worse, he couldn't mention the notes to Ignacio because the two had never discussed the subject of homosexuality. Ignacio seemed almost asexual to Lucas. Even when Lucas caught a gaze of tenderness toward him, Lucas did not dare to assume that it was anything but brotherly love.

He began to suffer from insomnia and lost his appetite. Dark shadows grew under his eyes. One day during confession his Father confessor asked him, "Do you touch yourself, Lucas?"

"No, no, Father. I don't," he replied; he didn't like lying, but he had no choice if he wanted to go to the seminary.

The next question was, "Does Ignacio Gutiérrez touch you?"

"Of course not, Father," Lucas said, breathing a sigh of relief. At least he did not have to lie about that.

"Only God knows what the truth is about you two. And I'll let Him be the judge of that," the Father confessor said in a stern tone. "However, I must warn you: if you continue your unseemly intimacy with that boy, you risk not being asked to return to school next year. You might as well forget about becoming a priest."

From that day on, Lucas went to great lengths to avoid being alone with Ignacio. He told himself that as long as he didn't do anything forbidden with Ignacio, they were not in imminent danger. At mealtimes he moved to another table. At first, Ignacio would give him puzzled looks, but Lucas could not bring himself to talk about what had transpired during confession. After Lucas acted coldly toward him a few times, Ignacio stopped trying to make eye contact with him. Though he now felt a painful loneliness, Lucas did not try to make new friends. Eventually, he admitted to himself that the pain this imposed separation caused him meant that he loved Ignacio, and that *that* kind of love was forbidden to him.

A week before summer vacation began, Lucas ran into Ignacio in the hallway on the way to class. There were no other boys around. Ignacio put the palms of his hands on Lucas's shoulders and pinned him hard against the wall. "If you don't want to be my friend anymore, at least tell me why. What did I do to you?" His face was distorted by a rage that frightened Lucas. "Don't be a coward," Ignacio said loudly. "Tell me why you're doing this. You owe me an explanation."

Lucas hoped Ignacio would hit him: it would give him an excuse to end their friendship. His tears began to flow. Ignacio took his hands off Lucas. "Spare me your crocodile tears," he sneered, and walked away. Lucas wanted to run after Ignacio, grab him by an arm to try to explain why it was best for them not to be close anymore—at least not for the time being. But he stood frozen, silent.

The day before Lucas left for the summer, Father Superior called him to his office. Lucas's agitation increased as the hour of the appointment neared. His biggest fear was that he was going to be told he would not be invited back to Colegio San José. Once he was in the office and was asked to take a seat, Father Superior wasted no time with preambles: "Your closeness with Ignacio Gutiérrez has come to my attention. I must warn you that Gutiérrez is not a good influence on you." Lucas's mind began to spin so fast he couldn't understand a word Father Superior was saying. When the dizziness subsided, he heard, "That boy's tormented by some demon. I doubt he'll become a priest. The only reason we haven't sent him back to his parents is because he has the best grades in his class." Father Superior paused to stare at Lucas, who lowered his eyes and dared not look up for fear of what they might reveal about his true feelings for Ignacio.

"I don't think I need to remind you," Father Superior continued, "that there are many boys in Colombia who would give anything for a chance to study here on a scholarship. During the school vacation, I forbid you to write to Gutiérrez. Even if he gets in touch with you, you must ignore his letters—that is, if you want to return to our school after vacation. Is that clear?"

Lucas nodded.

"Look at me, look me in the eye, Lucas, and promise me you won't have any contact with Gutiérrez during vacation."

Lucas's heart was beating so fast he felt his throat closing. "I promise I won't, Father," he managed to say.

"Very well then," Father Superior replied, and dismissed him.

* * *

Sitting next to his mother on the bus ride home to Bogotá, Lucas tried to conceal his sadness. The day before he had overheard one of his classmates mentioning that Ignacio was going to spend the vacation at the school, working in exchange for room and board. Lucas assumed this was because Ignacio's parents couldn't afford to pay for his bus ticket back home. Lucas tried to answer Clemencia's questions about his education with enthusiasm. He didn't want her to think that he was having doubts about the path he had chosen—that would have been crushing for her. Lucas wished he could tell his mother cheerful anecdotes about school life, but all he wanted to say was, "*Mami*, I love Ignacio." Lucas had never before felt so lonely. All his life he had been able to confide in Clemencia. No matter what he told her, his mother always took his side. It was painful to have a secret he couldn't share with her, not because he was ashamed of the love he felt for Ignacio, but because he didn't want to hurt her. How could he explain to her the reason for his despondency?

Sensing his reluctance to chat about his studies, Clemencia said, "I have a surprise for you, Lucas. I wanted to save it until this moment. My new job with the flower export business pays better than working for the Americans." Her eyes shone with pride. "You're not going back to Cousin Ema's house. She has some health problems and has decided to return to the Llanos to live close to her family. I've rented a little house in Suba. It's a town in the mountains just half an hour away from the city, and there's good public transportation. From now on, you'll have your own room always waiting for you in our house."

Ignacio smiled, leaned over, and kissed her cheek. "Thank you, Mami."

Clemencia went on, "Who knew that the experience I acquired on the farm taking care of the flowers we sold would come in handy one day!" But her words seemed to trigger a sad memory and she became quiet. Ignacio was sure Clemencia was thinking about his sisters and how she had had no contact with them after she'd left Güicán. His mother stared out the window until she eventually nodded off.

As the bus passed by farms, small towns, and food stands on the side of the road, Lucas kept hearing a voice in his head that repeated, *Ignacio. Ignacio. Ignacio.* The faster the bus traveled, the louder Ignacio's name rang in his ears. The closer they got to Bogotá, the more violently he desired to escape his body to stop the guilt that racked him. He wished he could talk to Ignacio one more time to ask him for forgiveness for withdrawing his friendship. He had not only betrayed Ignacio but also himself. He became so emotional that he, too, closed his eyes, and pretended to sleep. The darkness was soothing; it muffled his anguish. *When it's so dark,* he thought, *nothing in the world can remind me of him.*

"You're a little man now," Clemencia told Lucas when he turned fourteen that summer. "You're old enough to go downtown on your own to pay the utilities. It would be a big help to me."

He was happy to be of help to his mother and also excited to go do something in the city for the first time by himself.

The second time he was in downtown Bogotá doing

errands, Lucas noticed groups of boys his age walking on Carrera Séptima in flamboyant clothes, laughing and giggling loudly, throwing shameless looks at some of the men they passed. These boys frightened Lucas, but a part of him was also desperate to talk to them. However, he knew that if he associated with them he'd risk being labeled as one of them.

The next time Lucas was in the city, one of the street boys asked him as he went by, "Want to hang out with us?"

"No thanks," he replied hastily, avoiding eye contact. "I have to get back home."

"Don't look so scared, sister," the boy scoffed. "It's not like I invited you to sniff glue with us."

The brazen behavior of these boys fascinated and repelled Lucas. Once, he followed them at a distance all the way to Parque Nacional, where they sat on the lawn smoking a pipe in a spot sheltered by weeping willows. He had seen a TV program about hooligans who smoked crack and terrorized people. Lucas decided he wouldn't have anything to do with them and walked as fast as he could to the bus stop.

In Suba there was a Casa de la Cultura, where neighborhood young people gathered for cultural activities. Their drama club was in the middle of rehearsing a play they were going to put on at Christmastime. Lucas attended performances of boys and girls who recited their own poems or the works of José Asunción Silva, Porfirio Barba Jacob, Federico García Lorca, and other Colombian poets.

Clemencia encouraged Lucas to take advantage of the classes offered at the cultural center for a small fee.

She had heard that the young people who went there did
not belong to gangs or do drugs. Lucas started spending
his afternoons in the Casa de la Cultura, watching the
young people dancing and rehearsing plays. He remembered fondly the time he had taken dance lessons before
he went off to Colegio San José, so he ended up enrolling
in a dance class. In Suba, Lucas learned the steps of pa-
sillos and bambucos, peasant dances he had seen people
in Güicán perform in the plaza during festivals. But his
favorite was the *mapalé*, an Afro-Colombian dance that
had originated on Colombia's Atlantic coast. Lucas loved
what happened to him when he danced the mapalé: when
he leaped, he would try in his mind to stretch that moment into infinity, and for that nanosecond he'd feel he
could leave the world and travel up and up, higher and
higher, faster and faster, until planet earth became a small
blue ball. Then, with his legs, torso, head, arms, hands,
fingers, and toes, he would try to express what he felt at
that moment. He dreamed of becoming a good dancer so
that his mother could see him perform. When they finished rehearsing a dance, and he returned, panting, to the
world, for an instant Lucas would believe he had created
something beautiful and unique. It was as if another person had performed, not himself. Sometimes he wondered
if what he experienced was something like the ecstasy of
the saints when they were in God's presence and inundated
with His light.

A few days later, after he'd started taking dance classes,
as Lucas was leaving the center to go back home to make
dinner—he had learned simple recipes from watching
Clemencia in the kitchen—he heard a voice call, "Hey,
Lucas!"

He turned around and saw one of the other dancers from class; he was taller than the other boys, willowy, and black. Lucas had seen him dancing and practicing, and was impressed with his physical grace and beauty.

"My name's Julio. I see you all the time watching us practice."

They shook hands.

"My mother told me about you," Julio said. "She said your mother told her you want to become a priest. But you're a talented dancer. Maybe you'll be like that singing nun—a dancing priest!" He laughed at his own joke.

Lucas made a face at Julio and began to move away from him.

"I'm sorry I said that. That was stupid. We should be friends. Our mothers work at the same place, and we're neighbors."

Lucas thought Julio was a bit fresh, but he wasn't upset with him. Though his manner was gentle, Julio wasn't effeminate, so there was no danger in hanging out with him. *Besides*, Lucas thought, *I'm not physically attracted to him.*

From that afternoon on, Lucas walked home with Julio at the end of the day. Often, he invited Julio in for a glass of juice. They discovered they enjoyed playing checkers and Parcheesi. Lucas often felt tension in the air, but he wasn't interested in taking the first step.

After they had played Parcheesi on a few occasions, Julio said, "I'm bored playing these games. Let me show you something. Do you have any old newspapers?"

Lucas handed him some papers from the neatly stacked piles in the kitchen.

Julio said, "Follow me." In the living room, he spread

the newspapers on the floor. He sat on one of the chairs, unbuckled his pants, undid his zipper, and took out his erect cock.

Lucas suddenly felt as aroused as the first time he had masturbated while thinking about Ignacio.

"Get comfortable," Julio told him. "I play this game with my cousins."

Lucas unbuckled his belt and then stopped. Julio motioned with his hand for him to take out his penis. It was hard—Lucas's tension was almost overpowering.

Julio said, "Think of any girl you like and then we'll shoot and see whose cum lands farthest."

This became a daily ritual. After they masturbated, they'd throw the newspapers in the trash. Though they didn't touch, Lucas felt awful that he was engaging in such an activity with a man in his mother's house, while she was at work.

As if to make up for what he thought was his betrayal, Lucas worked hard at preparing dinner for Clemencia. She had one cookbook, and Lucas found that if he followed a recipe, the food turned out fine. After they ate, he always insisted on washing the dishes. Doing things for her made him feel less guilty.

"You're the best son any mother could wish for," she would often say.

Her compliments were like a nail hammered into his heart.

At night, Clemencia watched the Colombian soap operas for hours. Lucas found them ridiculous, but he enjoyed them nonetheless, following the story line along with her and paying attention when she explained a character's background. Keeping her company at night made him feel better because she seemed so happy spending time with him. She liked it when he stood behind her rocking chair and gently scratched her head.

Lucas could tell that she was often sad; she would sometimes look at pictures of Lercy and Adela and make dresses for one of their dolls, which she had taken with her when she left the farm. He knew Clemencia tried to get news about them from her acquaintances in Güicán. He understood that she never contacted his sisters directly because she feared Gumersindo could show up one day at their home in Suba and take him away, just to punish her.

Lucas would have done anything to see his mother smile more often. But he got the impression she had given up on ever finding any happiness on earth. It was a heavy burden for him to be her only source of joy.

Before going to bed, Clemencia always took a hot shower. Afterward, she chatted on the phone with her cousin Ema, or with a friend from work, before she turned off the light on her night table.

Lucas often wondered if this was the way most people lived.

There was one movie house in Suba: El Rex. At school in Facatativá, the TV set was kept locked in a closet and brought out only on Saturday nights so the students and teachers could watch movies on the VCR and on Sunday afternoons for soccer games. Lucas looked forward to the weekly movies, which were a break from the monotony of their studies. Most of the movies they saw were about the Christians martyred in Roman times, though now and then an American comedy would be slipped in. When the movies were more contemporary, the stories usually included nuns and priests. Lucas became obsessed with *A Nun's Story*: he fantasized that, after he was ordained, he would be sent to the jungle (like Audrey Hepburn in the movie) and there he would meet a doctor as handsome as Peter Finch, and they would fall in love with each other and live together forever in the jungle, taking care of the lepers.

In Suba, El Rex showed new movies. As Lucas passed by the movie house on his way to the Casa de la Cultura, he'd often stop to gaze at the posters advertising the current releases and forthcoming attractions. He also noticed that mostly men bought tickets for the three o'clock show and that they entered the theater in a hurry, as if they didn't want to be seen going in. A movie called *Philadelphia* was announced and was advertised as a story about AIDS. Lucas had read a few sketchy articles in the press about AIDS, a terrifying disease in the United States that targeted homosexuals.

Before Clemencia went to sleep one night, Lucas asked her if he could go to the movies.

She gave him the money for the ticket and added, "But you come straight home after the movie is over. Is that understood?"

Lucas cried through most of *Philadelphia*. He took the story as a warning of what could happen to him if he had sex with men—he would become infected and die a horrible death like the character played by Tom Hanks, whose comedies Lucas loved.

In the movie theater men performed oral sex on each other while pretending to watch the movie; in the smelly and filthy restroom he saw men engaging in sex. A couple of them exposed themselves and tried to touch Lucas, but he bolted out of the bathroom. After that experience, he waited until he got home to use the bathroom.

During that school vacation in Suba, more horrific stories began appearing on television and in the newspapers about men dying of AIDS. Clemencia had told him about the son of one of her coworkers who had recently died of the disease. "The worst thing that can happen to a mother is to lose one of her children," she said. "But to die of that disease is the absolute worst, Lucas. It's horrible how the other people at work shun her, as if *she* had the disease. It breaks my heart to see that."

Lucas prayed fervently to God to remove his overpowering desires for men. He went to Mass first thing in the morning and to confession every week. But he was careful about what he confessed to the priest.

All this time, Lucas never stopped thinking about Ignacio. He wondered how he was doing living with the brothers. He longed to hear Ignacio's voice and couldn't forgive himself for pulling back when he knew that Ignacio had no other friends in school. When Lucas least expected it—at Mass, in dance classes, or even when he masturbated with Julio—Ignacio's face would pop into his mind; he frequently dreamed about him as well. The dreams where Ignacio appeared were always sexual, and Lucas would wake up in the morning with an erection. Or worse, he'd wake to find he'd ejaculated during the night.

In his confusion, Lucas wondered whether the best thing for him might be to kill himself. At least this would spare Clemencia the shame of a homosexual son who died from AIDS. Lucas was sure that if he continued seeing Julio and going to the movies, it was inevitable he would end up having sex with men and die of the disease.

In the remaining weeks of his vacation, he started taking kung fu lessons, hoping they would make him act more masculine. He was aware that in the coming year at Colegio San José it would be hard to practice the vow of chastity. Yet he was desperate to go back to school, because life outside had no rules he was compelled to obey.

As the day of his departure grew closer, Lucas accepted that going back to Colegio San José meant having to resolve his feelings for Ignacio. But he didn't care, because more than anything else he longed to see his friend, even from afar. *I just want to hear his voice*, he'd say to himself. *And to smell him.*

The day he arrived back in Facatativá, Lucas didn't see Ignacio around. *Had he been sent home to his parents?* he wondered. Ignacio would not have chosen to leave the school of his own accord.

Lucas waited to see if Ignacio would appear, and when he did not, Lucas figured it might be safe to ask another student where Ignacio had disappeared to. The student didn't know what had happened; but the next day, when they sat next to each other for the evening meal, he said under his breath, "Gutiérrez was sent to a seminary in the Putumayo jungle. Father Superior didn't want him here anymore. He'll be there for the rest of his novitiate." Then, with a mischievous grin, he added, "Are you prepared to remain a virgin until you see him again, princess?"

Only after the other students had left Colegio San José for summer vacation had Ignacio begun to acknowledge how hurt he was by the cold and abrupt way in which Lucas had ended their friendship. He suspected that Lucas had been pressured to sever their bond, but it was hard to forgive him nonetheless. He missed Lucas with an ache that was almost physical, yet he couldn't hate him. He was the only close friend Ignacio had ever had, and his presence in the seminary had made life bearable for him.

He experienced a harsh new loneliness—finding someone to love and then losing him. He could no longer deny his romantic feelings for Lucas. From the moment they'd met, Ignacio had been aware of the way Lucas looked at him, his brown eyes shining with longing. This had frightened him so much that he'd constantly reminded himself to conceal what he felt for Lucas.

Ignacio knew that his sharp tongue rubbed his teachers the wrong way and that if they started to gossip about his sexuality, he would end up getting expelled from school, putting an end to his aspirations to go as far away as possible from the remote mountains where he'd been born.

Ignacio's chores included cleaning the bathrooms, sweeping and mopping the floors, chopping vegetables for the meals, washing dishes, helping with the laundry and ironing, attending five a.m. Mass every day, and dusting the books in the library. He loved handling the books, reading random pages, looking for a subject to capture his interest. Sometimes he would get so engrossed reading he'd forget that he was supposed to be working. His ignorance overwhelmed him. There had been no books in his parents' home, but in school he discovered that reading expanded his mind, and the more he read, the more clearly he could think and express himself, not only in writing but also in his speech—and this gave him an advantage over the other boys his age. Each book he touched held, he thought, a key to satiate his hunger for knowledge and answers to all the questions he had about life.

Ignacio loved the silence of the library. One afternoon he was reading at the long table when Father Daniel came in. Of all his teachers, this man was the friendliest, and Ignacio was drawn to his affable manner—a quality he knew he himself lacked. Ignacio was also held rapt by the teacher's quick intelligence; in his world history classes, Father Daniel talked about many books and subjects that Ignacio knew nothing about. While the other teachers did not deviate from the textbooks they taught, Father Daniel would draw connections among different historical periods and often went off on a tangent about the literature, painting, and architecture of that time. When he talked about major historical figures, he didn't just tell you the names of the battles they had won, or how long they were in power—he would discuss their psychology, their existential struggles. Ignacio longed to one day know as much as his teacher.

Father Daniel greeted him and asked, "Do you come to the library often?"

"Yes, Father," Ignacio replied, nodding. "It's part of my duties," he added in a defensive tone.

"What kinds of books do you like to read?"

Ignacio's face grew warm; he was mortified that he was blushing. "I love reading books about history. My favorite historical figure is Joan of Arc." When Father Daniel remained quiet, Ignacio hastened to say, "I like that she sacrificed herself for the French people."

ied in literature classes, Father. I can't say I much like the poems we've read."

"Maybe you need to read contemporary poetry."

Ignacio was puzzled. He thought all poetry was old.

The following day, Father Daniel handed him a copy of *Marilyn Monroe, and Other Poems*. "The author, Ernesto Cardenal, is a priest and a poet," Father Daniel said. Ignacio had seen photos of the famous actress.

"You might like these poems; you won't be bored, I promise. Anyway, it won't hurt you to read Father Cardenal's poetry."

Ignacio was surprised to discover that there were priests who wrote about movie stars—especially one he had seen naked in a photograph on an old calendar in a grocery store in El Carmen, the town near to where his parents lived. Before he arrived at Colegio San José, he hadn't seen very many movies. In El Carmen movies were shown only on Saturday nights. The town was about two kilometers from home and he and his sisters had to make the long walk in the dark, which was dangerous. Movies cost money, so they were only allowed to go once a year, after the school year was over, and only if they got good grades.

On the back of the volume of poems Ignacio read that Father Cardenal lived in Nicaragua, in Solentiname, an island in Lake Nicaragua where there was a community of monks. He read all the poems in a couple of days, some of them several times. He especially liked the long poem about Marilyn Monroe, which made him sad for her. When Ignacio returned the book, he said that he had liked the poems, and then asked Father Daniel if he'd ever been to Solentiname.

Father Daniel smiled. "Yes, she was a great patriot."

Ignacio thought it was strange that Father Daniel had praised Joan of Arc for her patriotism, not for her saintliness. Could it mean that to Father Daniel politics and the war against the English invaders were more important than Joan's connection to God?

Ignacio was in the habit of going to the library around four in the afternoon. After that first encounter with Father Daniel, the two kept running into each other: they would exchange courteous greetings and retreat to opposite ends of the room. Father Daniel wore glasses and would sit on a cushioned chair near a window to read, occasionally looking up from the book at the cuckoo clock on the wall. Now and then he would pause to make a remark about the afternoon drizzle that was a daily occurrence in Facatativá during that time of the year. Ignacio found himself stealing glances. Father Daniel was a beanpole, the youngest of the teachers in Colegio San José. His manners were refined; his long hands looked as if they were made of the smoothest porcelain; his thick brown hair was parted in the middle and cut short at the back of his neck. As he read, he'd brush his hair back with the three middle fingers of his right hand.

Weeks went by in this manner and Ignacio began to think they might never become better acquainted, until one day Father Daniel stopped at Ignacio's place at the table as he was leaving. After they had exchanged pleasantries, he asked, "Do you like poetry?"

Ignacio wanted to say something that would please his teacher, but instead the truth came out of his lips: "I haven't read many poems other than the ones we've stud-

"No, I haven't. Did you know the priests who live there are involved in liberation theology?"

Ignacio shuffled his feet. He wasn't sure what that term meant and was too ashamed to admit his ignorance.

"They are priests who wanted to help create a new Catholic church that serves the poor," Father Daniel explained. "That's not what we teach at Colegio San José. Our brothers here are old-school."

Ignacio began to daydream about Solentiname. He tried to imagine what the place looked like and how the monks dressed. The next time they chatted, Ignacio asked Father Daniel if he wanted to go live in Solentiname.

"I think I've been called to do my work here in this school, teaching you boys. I'm happiest when I'm in the classroom." He paused. "Why do you ask? Would you like to visit Solentiname someday?"

"It sounds like a nice place," Ignacio said. "I've never been on an island."

He sensed there was something Father Daniel was withholding from him, but he didn't dare pry. It was not, after all, as if they were friends. But Ignacio couldn't help wonder if Father Daniel was involved in some way with liberation theology. Ignacio had heard about revolutionary priests who had joined the communist guerrilla group ELN to fight against the government. Despite his political naïveté, he understood that the priests in Facatativá were not interested in revolution, much less Communist revolutionaries, which was how he had heard the members of the ELN described by his teachers, who seemed to be only focused on strictly adhering to Catholic doctrine. Ignacio wanted to know more about the Solentiname priests, but he told himself he should be patient. Perhaps then Father

Daniel might eventually consider him a friend and answer his questions.

Growing up on a farm, Ignacio had heard his father routinely curse the rich landowners, who were in cahoots with the government to keep the poor hungry and ignorant. In the world outside the farm, Ignacio had seen Indians like himself (descendants of the Motilones, who had scalped Spaniards in an earlier time) treated as incapable of becoming "civilized." Indians always had to defer to the white people in town, on the roads, on the sidewalks, even in church—where whites sat up front and Indians in the back. A few times in town, as he walked down the street, children had come to the windows of their homes and yelled, "Indian, take your syphilis back to the jungle!"

Ignacio didn't dare ask his father why strangers accused him of having syphilis. The textbooks he studied at school didn't address the topic, and due to his father's limited understanding, Ignacio knew he could not discuss these subjects with him. Before long, he too began to hate the government, the rich landowners, and white people.

Ignacio had never discussed his vocation honestly with a priest, and wished he could air his doubts about the path his parents had chosen for him. He realized that for someone of humble origins like himself, the priesthood was one of the few means of getting an education. He was also painfully aware that religion did not assuage his anxiety about his ignorance. Sometimes he wished that he had the peasant mind-set that if you suffered in this life, if you sacrificed and accepted God's will for you, you would get your reward in heaven—and nothing else mattered. But his bouts of religiosity, his periods of blind faith, would last only a day or two—and then he'd again be filled with doubts and dissatisfaction.

Other than Lucas—who had listened to him sympathetically but was not intellectually curious by nature—Ignacio didn't know anyone who cared about his future. Also, he was aware that no matter how much he and Lucas liked each other, nothing could change the fact that he was an Indian and Lucas was a white-looking mestizo.

As the weeks passed, and he continued to see Father Daniel in the library, Ignacio considered being truthful with his teacher. He was desperate to be shown a way out of his ignorance and confusion. It troubled him that at the mere sight of Father Daniel, he became increasingly agitated. *Should he have a talk with his teacher about his predicament or keep his doubts to himself as he always had*, he wondered. The next time they ran into each other in the library, he told himself, he would try to engage Father Daniel in this conversation.

That very afternoon Father Daniel came into the library as Ignacio was reshelving books. He waved and smiled, as he always did, then sat by the window. As he was putting on his reading glasses, Ignacio hurried to his side and said, "Father, I need your advice." His hands were trembling, so he locked his fingers behind his back.

"Yes, of course. How can I help you, Ignacio?"

He began to sputter words that were so thick in his throat they were choking him. "I have doubts about . . . my vocation, Father. I like studying and learning new things, but I'm on this religious path to please my parents." He stopped there—afraid to reveal too much.

Father Daniel stared at him, silent, yet from his expression Ignacio could tell he didn't judge him harshly.

It was almost as if his teacher saw something Ignacio couldn't see about himself. A force stronger than his instinct for self-protection made him add, "Father, I'm not sure I believe in God, either. What I like about becoming a priest is the idea of helping people."

His teacher became thoughtful. "I wonder, Ignacio," he began, "if it's a requisite to believe in God to help people get close to Him. If you have the vocation to help those who suffer, it means you've been blessed with that gift. I'd like to think that God has no vanity. Maybe God cares more about that than about us believing in Him. To become a priest it might be enough simply to follow the example of Jesus Christ."

Though Father Daniel's words did not quiet the turmoil in Ignacio's mind, they gave him something new to think about. He was still full of doubts, but his future no longer looked like it had to be a shameful lie—pretending to be someone he was not. For the first time in his life, he had a small bit of hope.

Ignacio had noticed that whenever he ran into Father Superior, the man would glare at him disapprovingly. He was particularly aware of this dislike one afternoon when Father Superior wandered into the library and found Ignacio and Father Daniel chatting. Father Superior immediately came up with an errand for Ignacio—as if he couldn't stand the thought of the two of them being together. After that encounter, Ignacio sensed that Father Superior was always watching him. With no other students around, the tension escalated rapidly. Ignacio decided that unless Father Superior forbade him to talk to Father Daniel, he would seize any chance he had to speak with him. Their brief exchanges made his loneliness less raw; he was thrilled that an adult he admired took an interest in him. But Ignacio was distressed that in his dreams, he and his teacher kissed and made love. Those dreams saturated the hours of the day too. *He's only interested in teaching me about poetry and Colombian politics*, Ignacio would repeat to himself. *That's all.* But what if it was love—that feeling that was often expressed in the poems and a few of the novels they'd studied in the seminary? Whatever it was, it was the most powerful feeling he had ever experienced before, because it was not just sexual—as it was with Lucas, whom he now admitted to himself he'd wanted to touch and possess.

Shortly before the new semester began, Father Superior called Ignacio to his office. Because he had been asked to visit the office on only a couple of occasions, Ignacio knew that something of consequence was about to happen. Father Superior invited him to sit down and immediately got to the point.

"Ignacio, after consulting with the other brothers here, we've decided that you should continue your religious education in the seminary in the town of Palos de la Quebrada, in the Putumayo. You can finish your high school there and then begin your novitiate. If everything goes well, you'll go to university before you get ordained. Good luck to you, Ignacio. You'll be provided with everything you need for your trip." With a wave of his hand, he indicated that their meeting was over.

Palos de la Quebrada. Ignacio recognized the name as soon as Father Superior had said it. He must have been about ten years old when he saw a newspaper photo of a massacre that had taken place there. Without knowing

it, Father Superior was exiling Ignacio to live inside an
image that had haunted him.

He kept busy all day so he didn't have time to think,
but when he took his walk in the courtyard at the end of
the day, the news began to sink in. It was common knowledge that aspiring seminarians whose vocation was sus-
pect, or about whom it was thought the strict discipline of
priestly life might be too much, were sent to inhospitable
places where they would be physically, psychologically,
and spiritually tested. No matter what happened to him,
Ignacio told himself, there was no going back to his parents' farm—no fate could be more depressing than that.
He thought it was unfair he was being punished for being
argumentative about Catholic precepts, but he would do
the best he could with the path that had been laid out for
him. From that moment on, Ignacio decided he would
wrap himself in an invisible cloak that concealed his true
feelings.

The photo that had haunted him since childhood
had been published under the headline, "FARC Massacres Boys." The photo showed a mass of rotten, bloated
corpses of adolescent boys floating on the surface of a
small lagoon in the Putumayo jungle, near Palos de la
Quebrada. The article reported in stark language that
forty-eight boys, between the ages of twelve and sixteen,
had been killed by the FARC guerrillas because they had
refused to march off with them into the jungle.

Each boy had been shot in the forehead. In the photo
it looked as if they all had a third eye staring lifelessly at
the unconcerned sky. There were no vultures in the picture. Had they been shot at to keep them away from the
carrion until after the pictures were taken for the press?

Who had taken the photos—the army? The guerrillas?

Ignacio didn't cut the picture out of the newspaper: the image was instantly etched in his brain. He started having nightmares about the dead boys with their distended bellies trapped in a lake of coagulated blood. He never mentioned the photo to anyone; its gruesome power forced him into silence. He feared that if he talked about it he would lessen the horror of what had happened and that would somehow make him complicit. In his nightmares, the dead children parted their stiff purple lips and chanted a mournful tune Ignacio had sung in childhood games: "*Mambrú went off to war—oh what pain, what pain, what sorrow.*" Over and over, the dead children uttered these lyrics. In the background, he heard a macabre buzz of frenzied flesh-eating flies.

On his last day in Facatativá, while walking with Father Daniel during the hour of recess before dinner, Ignacio informed him of his imminent departure.

"I didn't know you were being sent to the Putumayo," Father Daniel said, looking surprised. He stopped walking and put a hand on Ignacio's shoulder. "I will miss you."

Ignacio took those four words as a terse admission of Father Daniel's affection for him. They made him happier than he had been since first meeting Lucas.

"In some fundamental way the community where you're going may not be very different from this school," Father Daniel said. "But in the Putumayo there's no way to ignore that Colombia *is* at war. Here in Facatativá we're so close to Bogotá that it's almost as if the war is happening in a foreign country. I want you to keep your eyes open—which I know you will do—and think about what you see. But be careful what you say to anyone, and whom you trust, until you understand the world you'll be living in. In particular, mind what you say to the people outside the seminary. Until you understand the situation, promise me you'll keep your opinions to yourself."

The seriousness of these words alarmed Ignacio. "I will, Father."

"Maybe the doubts that you have about your vocation will be answered in the Putumayo. Listen carefully to your conscience and your true calling will be revealed."

Later, as they were heading in the direction of the main building, Father Daniel put his hand on Ignacio's wrist. "I'd like to stay in touch with you. If you like, we can correspond. I promise to tell you things that right now we don't have the time to go into. I will pray for you, Ignacio." As they entered the dining hall, Father Daniel blessed him before they went off in separate directions.

Ignacio remained awake that night, deeply fearful of this drastic change in his life. The next day, when he boarded the bus bound for the jungle, Father Daniel's promise to write to him was still ringing in his ears, and it was enough to make him feel he was not alone in the world.

CHAPTER THREE
THE PUTUMAYO
1994

THE JOURNEY BY BUS FROM FACATATIVÁ to Palos de la Quebrada took over twenty-four hours, traveling on dusty roads. Ignacio had to change buses twice and noticed that the passengers on each bus eyed one another suspiciously. As the hours passed and the Andes faded behind them, leaving the coolness of the mountains painted with emerald hues to enter the metallic-green jungle with its stupefying heat and humidity, Ignacio became covered in sweat and was stung by pertinacious mosquitoes. On both sides of the road, behind the wall of vegetation, lay an inscrutable world. One-horse towns with names like Mocoa, Puerto Asis, and Puerto Leguízamo appeared on the borders of the jungle, breaking up the monotony. The bus crossed bridges over the waters of the Putumayo, Caquetá, Orito, San Miguel, and Macayá rivers. Ignacio was hearing many of these names for the first time. For the first time, too, he saw the Quichuas, Ingas, Sionas, and Vitotos Indians who lived in protected areas. Ignacio had heard at school that these Indian communities welcomed the evangelical missionaries, who competed with the Catholic church in proselytizing the locals. These religious groups, in the absence of government agencies, helped the displaced people who had been forced to abandon their homes in the jungle.

The bus moved past oil refineries that sent up foul jets of smoke, blackening large areas of the sky. The workers lived in wood shacks inside sprawling compounds that were hemmed in by barbed wire and littered with plastic and glass bottles, metal containers, and heaps of garbage where vultures fought for scraps. On sandy clearings along the muddy rivers, Ignacio observed men digging and panning for gold. Sometimes, when rays of sunlight hit the strainers the miners used to sift the metal from the sand and water, golden flashes fleetingly blinded him. In places where the miners had already finished looking for gold, there were yawning craters, as if meteorites had crashed into the earth. Ignacio saw large fields being burned for cultivation or for raising cattle. The bus traveled for many miles before he saw a wild animal crossing the road, or even a bird flying. The emaciated Indians who sold fruit and water on the roadside looked with glazed eyes at the travelers. Occasionally, in the distant mountains, bright green patches of land were visible where the coca plant was cultivated.

The detritus of war was everywhere: rivers choked with crude oil, spilled from pipelines blown up by the guerrillas. Bloated carcasses of animals coursed along the oil-thick waters. The stench of rotting flesh was overpowering. The passengers who stared straight ahead stoically, Ignacio decided, were the locals; the newcomers to the region, like himself, stuck their heads out of the open windows to retch.

During the excruciatingly long hours on the bus, Ignacio reflected on how his life had turned into an ongoing journey with unknown destinations. Where, and when, would his travels stop? Each new geographic move was another step distancing him farther from the world of his parents.

The second day on the bus, as the sun set, the sky for a few minutes turned a bright crimson that made Ignacio think of a ceiling painted with fresh blood. When darkness fell, many passengers took out their rosaries and began to pray. The passengers spoke in whispers; when they talked to someone across the aisle, their voices quavered and their gestures were jumpy. Ignacio wanted to fall asleep and wake up when the bus arrived in Palos de la Quebrada, but his fear of what might happen under the cover of night kept him awake.

As the bus barreled down the road in the darkness, some passengers suddenly cried out and jerked away from their windows, pointing at severed heads hanging from the vegetation that canopied the thoroughfare. Each time the low-hanging heads bumped against the roof of the bus or brushed against the windows, smearing the surface of the glass, the passengers would shriek again.

Despite the terror that gripped him, Ignacio forced himself to keep his eyes closed; eventually, he fell asleep. When he woke up, the sun was rising, and his fellow passengers were quiet, but they looked as if they hadn't slept all night. To his great relief, the horror of nighttime on the road in the Putumayo had dissipated.

The bus came to a stop in front of a wooden house where people had gathered. Ignacio was the only passenger who got off at Palos de la Quebrada. He had been told before he left Colegio San José that the seminary in the Putumayo had been notified of the day of his arrival. After the conductor handed him his suitcase, Ignacio real-

ized that nobody had come to meet him. The locals stared
at him suspiciously, so he made an effort to hide his dis-
tress. Ignacio approached a man seated behind a table
on the sidewalk. He looked like the person who sold bus
tickets. Ignacio smiled and said, "Good morning, sir. Can
you point me in the direction of the seminary." The man's
gaze of hostility abruptly softened and the people around
him seemed to accept Ignacio's presence in the town.

He was pointed toward a path that wandered away
from the village. Seemingly impenetrable jungle bordered
both sides of the sandy path. He crossed a soccer field
strewn with pebbles and prickly nettles. In the distance he
could see a wooden church among a scattering of buildings with thatched roofs. Though it was still early in the
morning, Ignacio's shirt was already drenched in sweat,
so he walked as fast as he could to reach the place where
his vocation would be tested for the next five years.

The numbing heat that drained his energy, the asphyxiat-
ing humidity, being drenched in sweat during the hottest
hours of the day, the nightly torment of the mosquitoes—
all these took some time getting used to. The twenty-five
brothers in the community were friendly and helpful, but
there was so much to learn that everything went by in a
blur. Other than his chats with Father Daniel, there was
nothing Ignacio missed about Colegio San José. He was
eager to see what life in Palos would hold for him.

At irregular intervals during the day, and with regularity at night, single gunshots were interspersed with the
rattling cacophony of machine guns. The gunfire sounded
like it was coming from nearby. Ignacio noticed he was
the only one in the seminary who seemed distracted by

the sounds. Was the army doing target practice? One afternoon gunfire suddenly went off as he was walking in
the yard with Iván, a tall black seminarian who had be-
friended him. In two more years, Iván would be graduating and leaving the Putumayo.

Iván chuckled when he saw Ignacio shudder. "That,
by the way," he said, "is the soundtrack in this place.
Relax—most of the time those aren't real shots. The guerrillas play tapes of gunfire through loudspeakers hidden
in the jungle lest people forget we're in a war zone. It's
their way of keeping everyone in a state of constant fear."
He paused, letting Ignacio digest this. "But sometimes the
machine-gun fire is from the police or the army shooting
at the guerrillas. It's the government's way of reminding people that the Colombian armed forces are here in
the region. After a while you'll become immune to those
sounds and you'll begin to think of the gunshots as the
equivalent of frantic drums in the background during
Tarzan movies."

Ignacio laughed, though he had never seen a Tarzan
movie. Iván's matter-of-fact explanation unsettled him,
but remembering Brother Daniel's advice to speak with
caution, he didn't ask any questions.

Ignacio followed, to the letter, the strict routines, and
soon he found comfort in their numbing mindlessness.
He awoke with the first tolling of the bell at four a.m.
Sweaty and sticky, he was still half-asleep as he rushed
to the communal bathrooms to shower. By five o'clock,
refreshed by the cold water, he was dressed and waiting
in the chapel for the heavy-eyed dawdlers.

Afterward, on their knees, the community observed a

period of silence for an hour. When they left the chapel
the tops of the trees were dabbed in the pink light of the
rising sun and a riotous chorus of birdsong greeted them.
It was Ignacio's favorite time of day, because it was still
cool and the morning music cheered him.

He marched off to attend to his duties, which included
watering the vegetable gardens, helping with the milking
of four cows, and removing fresh eggs from the chicken
coops. He liked that one week he would help to cook,
another week he'd sweep the floors, or keep the chapel
spotless, or wash and iron clothes, or make sure that the
large earthenware jars standing in the cool shady corners of the buildings were filled with water from the well.
Twice a day he would poke a stick into the damp corners
beneath the water vessels to make sure no scorpions were
hiding there. On his parents' farm there were scorpions
everywhere. Since they liked to crawl into shoes at night,
Ignacio and his siblings had slept with their shoes on,
or placed them under their pillows. After he arrived in
Facatativá, he thought he'd never have to deal with scorpions again. But in Palos, every night before he got into
bed, he checked for the venomous pests beneath his pillow and blanket.

By the time he'd arrive at the refectory at seven fifteen, Ignacio was weak with hunger. Father Superior sat
at the head of the table, with the novitiates taking their
assigned seats. A friar would read aloud for ten minutes about the life of a saint. When Father Superior said,
"Enough," they'd recite a prayer of thanks for the day's
food, and then have one cup of *café con leche* each, a
piece of the coarse dry cassava bread that the Indians
ate, and some days, as a special treat, a banana. After

they had finished their breakfast, Father Superior would remark, "Thank you, God, for the holy hands that prepared our meal." Ignacio would laugh like everyone else, but he had to struggle not to roll his eyes.

He succeeded in hiding his boredom during the morning classes in liturgy and ornamentation, where they learned about the various objects used for Mass, which linens were considered sacred, how to pour the sacramental wine, and when a certain prayer was said. He dutifully learned everything involved in the Mass ritual, but he looked forward to the classes in theology, the humanities, and philosophy—subjects which the seminary took pride in teaching from a secular point of view. In the afternoons, the seminarians studied psychology, Spanish literature, and Latin, which Ignacio also enjoyed. He decided to throw himself into his studies. The sameness of the days in the seminary was somewhat relieved by the strict academic routines because they made the hours go faster. He found consolation in reminding himself that in a few years he would be able to go to university, perhaps in Bogotá.

A bowl of soup for lunch was followed by an hour-long siesta. At this time of day, the heat was so intense that even the flies dozed off as the jungle fell silent. At five o'clock, when the heat had lessened, classes were over for the day. Then the seminarians were free to play soccer, go for walks, read, and get together to chat and play checkers, Parcheesi, or chess. It was the only time that was all their own. Dinner at five forty-five was invariably rice and red beans, and sometimes fried ripe plantains as well. For dessert they each got a slice of the salty white cheese with guava paste that was made in the seminary.

As they ate, the seminarians shared what they had done and learned that day.

Around six thirty villagers would begin arriving to the chapel to say evening prayers, which included reciting the rosary. Afterward, for an hour, the community played tapes of religious music. The music pouring out of the speakers in the bell tower served to momentarily drown out the gunfire echoing in the jungle. Before they went to bed, the seminarians said their prayers, kneeling in front of the altar in the chapel.

Instead of playing games with his classmates during his free hour, Ignacio began to go for short visits to Palos de la Quebrada. It was a dismal place, its inhabitants lethargic, as if crushed by the jungle. The main traffic on the road that crossed the town consisted of mules carrying goods and trucks loaded with timber. A bus stopped in the village every other day in front of the general store to drop off mail and merchandise to be consumed by the locals. Ignacio observed that people used the bus to travel away from Palos; it was a rare occasion when a passenger got off the bus to stay in the village. The townspeople got used to seeing Ignacio wandering about, and he enjoyed the laughter of children playing in the streets. When children called out, "Hello, Brother Ignacio," he smiled and waved. Sometimes they followed him as he walked around without talking to him. The older men playing dominoes under shady trees tipped their hats when he passed by.

The barefoot, half-naked Indians who traversed the road in both directions, looking as if they were sleepwalking, fascinated him. Their haunted expressions suggested a desperation to hurry out of the jungle, as if they were fleeing a plague. It seemed the only plan they had was to keep walking, until they had left the region behind.

Ignacio was cautious of the fully armed people wearing fatigues that crisscrossed the town's main street on mules. Whether they were guerrillas or paramilitaries, it was hard to tell. The Paleros regarded them all with fear. The strangers acted as if he were invisible; when they did take notice of him it was with a hostile stare.

In the company of other seminarians and teachers, Ignacio began to venture beyond Palos. He fell under the spell of the exuberance and beauty of the Putumayo region: the purling streams, their currents slowed by deep pools of still water; the roaring waterfalls, at the bottom of which lay ponds of cool transparent water, in which you could see fish as clearly as in an aquarium; the turbulent dark waters of the rivers, which hid treacherous currents; the flesh-eating fish and reptiles. Gigantic mesas (which the locals called *tepuis*) were the main features of this land: they rose up toward the sky like landing platforms for spacecraft. Everything in the jungle gave the appearance of being under a magnifying glass. The beauty of nature sometimes made him forget the unrelenting bugs, the parasites and worms in the water, and the poisonous vermin.

During the first weeks, the symphony of birdsong and calls—which began at dawn and reached its highest pitch around noon when the jungle seemed to burn silently in invisible flames—kept Ignacio in a daze. Frequently, clouds of confetti-colored birds crossed the sky in eerie silence. But a blue, cloudless sky could turn ominous in seconds. Torrential rains poured down without warning, forcing people and animals to seek refuge, sometimes for hours and sometimes for entire days.

It was harder to get used to the clatter of army helicopters hovering over the rooftops. From them, flyers rained down that said, *If you befriend a guerrilla or give them shelter, you'll be punished.* The most common flyers promised the Paleros monetary rewards for any guerrilla they turned in. Other flyers said, *Be a patriot. Denounce the guerrillas hiding among you. Join the army.*

One night, as Ignacio and the brothers were filing out of the refectory, the sound of barking dogs could be heard coming from Palos; cries of terror followed. The seminarians ran outside. What looked like balloons of fire fell from the helicopters; wherever they landed—on the trees, on a field, on the thatched roofs of homes—a voracious fire was ignited.

Ignacio stood petrified, bewildered by the spectacle of these globes of flame that kept falling from the sky. The frenzied barking of the dogs and the frightened cries of children, and people whose homes had been hit, punctured the silence of the night jungle.

During his walks alone, Ignacio experienced enough peace of mind to question the life he had chosen. He was waiting for some kind of religious awakening that would show him he was on the right path. Thus far the only convincing reason he could find for choosing to become a priest was that it was a way out of his parents' world of ignorance and poverty.

On one of his daily walks with Iván, Ignacio told him about seeing the photo of the massacre near Palos. "You

can imagine the terror I felt when Father Superior at Colegio San José announced I was being sent here."

Iván remained silent, but Ignacio was determined to
have at least one of his questions answered. "I tell you this
because you're my friend. I knew very little else about life
in the Putumayo. What's happening here?"

"Where have you been all your life?" Iván snorted.
"How could you be so ignorant about what's going on
in Colombia? You weren't living in a cave in the jungle."

"My parents couldn't read," Ignacio replied angrily.
"There was no electricity on the farm, so I never watched
television or listened to the radio. At Colegio San José
news of the outside world was banned. And here we are
isolated too."

"Ignacio, everyone in Colombia knows that the guerrillas and the paramilitaries levy 'taxes' on the peasants
and Indians in exchange for a promise to protect their
crops. Otherwise, the farmers have to sell their coca and
poppy harvests to the cartels, who pay the lowest prices."
Iván sighed, rolling his eyes. "Peasants get chicken feed,
barely enough to keep them from starvation. In other
words, the weak get screwed one way or another. You
understand it now?"

For the first time in his life Ignacio began to question seriously what it meant to him to be a Barí Indian.
Dressed as a seminarian he still looked Indian, but at least
he was treated with a respect that the semi-naked Indians
he saw in the Putumayo didn't get from the authorities or
the whites and mestizos. Ignacio was well aware that this
was because he had acquired the manners of an educated
white man and spoke Spanish without an accent.

When he observed the Indians who went through

Palos de la Quebrada and those in the communities he came across in the jungle, he was aware of the differences between himself and the natives whose contact with white people was limited. The indigenous people who had recently settled among whites regarded him with suspicion, if not outright mistrust, as if they considered him a man who had betrayed his own people and behaved as if he were superior to them.

Ignacio's family had left the remote settlements in the mountains just a few generations before he was born, to move closer to the schools, churches, hospitals, and jobs the whites could offer them. In turn, the Colombians, as the Barís referred to them, bought their agricultural products, the highly priced cacao in particular. They also purchased the crafts the Barís made, especially the women's embroidered cotton fabrics and the strings of colorful stones that they wrapped around their necks and wrists; these trinkets were popular souvenirs for foreigners who visited Colombia.

The Barís Ignacio had known growing up wanted their children to attend school, to learn the ways of the whites, to understand how their world worked. The Barís had always used ancestral remedies when they fell ill, but now they knew to seek treatment from white doctors if they did not recover. Yet, no matter how much he adopted the ways of the whites and mestizos, Ignacio felt that he could still only know them from the outside. And though it was forbidden by law to abuse the indigenous population or discriminate against them, Ignacio's people were seen as unknowable, incapable of assimilating fully into white Colombian culture. It was a painful conclusion for Ignacio.

Now and then he felt homesick for the Barí festivals, when families would gather in the countryside to dance, sing, get drunk on *chicha*, tell stories about their ancestors, and seek the advice of the *curanderos*, the medicine men who were revered because of the knowledge they had accumulated traveling from one horizon to the next.

Often the Barís sang songs that were simply lists of words they remembered in their language. Ignacio had vivid memories of the elders drinking potions made from hallucinogenic mushrooms and roots, and then sharing their visions around a bonfire.

In the month of August, his parents would bury offerings of flowers, fruit, candies, incense, aromatic woods, and rabbits and kid goats slaughtered in honor of Pachamama, the Earth Mother goddess. Later, Ignacio read that Pachamama was worshipped in the High Andes in Bolivia, Peru, Ecuador, and Chile; but in Colombia, only in the mountains in Norte de Santander where he grew up. These mountains were the last stretch of the Andes before the cordillera ended in Venezuela. In secrecy, as if they were afraid of still being considered savages, Ignacio's people had dotted the forested parts of their small farms with shrines made of rocks, feathers, animal bones, eggs, and bead necklaces, to appease and give thanks to the powerful deities who lived in the trees, rivers, ponds, streams, and under the ground.

Aside from those special occasions, Ignacio's parents were devout Catholics who went to Mass on Sunday, confessed, took communion, and baptized their children with Christian names. During the month of May, they honored the Virgin Mary, and the Virgin of Chiquinquirá, who was half Virgin Mary, half Pachamama.

After he went to study in Facatativá, Ignacio seldom thought about the Barí religion, not because he was
ashamed of his family's Indian customs, but because he
did not believe in their magical beings, just as he did not
believe there was a God. And yet he couldn't deny he
felt something like the presence of God in nature, in the
moon and the sun, in the elements of fire and water, and
especially in the wind. Though the Barí beliefs had become diluted over the centuries, he did not reject the no-
tion that people lived in a middle level—the one called
Earth. In this middle level, the most feared deity was Old
Man Wind, because He was responsible—when He was
angry—for sweeping away the clouds and creating periods of near starvation from drought. Old Man Wind was
also responsible for bringing new people into the middle
level, and for relocating those who needed to move on
to another life beyond the horizon. There, the rules of
life were the same as in the world they had just left, and
they were given a chance to begin again and avoid the
mistakes they had made in the last world. However, those
who had learned their lessons in the first world would
not have to move on to the next.

Ignacio came to accept that he would forever be divided
this way, so he determined to put behind the notions of
his childhood and live like a white man. He vowed not
to be ashamed of his Barí origins, but at the same time
accept that the world belonged to white people, and to
the mestizos, but that the Indians—of whatever ethnic
group—would always be seen as inferior.

Though it pained him not to know his own people,
Ignacio made it a point to stop looking at them as ignorant, uncivilized creatures, and to see them, instead, as a

tragically doomed people who were on the verge of disappearing and—worse, in his view—forgetting who they had been.

Two years went by, years that seemed exact replicas of each other due to the ongoing violence in the Putumayo. In order not to explode from anger, Ignacio closed his eyes to the widespread suffering. The days passed in jungle time, the hours dragging by like the sloths he saw inching up and down the high trees. His future graduation as a seminarian would be his only escape from the Putumayo.

Ignacio went to Mass, prayed, meditated, and kept silent when required. He hated that he did all these things mechanically—like brushing his teeth in the mornings. He tried hard to conform, not to voice his discontent, and to get along with everyone. Still, it was hard for him to feel kinship with his fellow novitiates, with their sheepish resignation and unquestioning minds.

He began to believe that every day he was at risk of being buried alive in a green chamber choked with vegetable matter and giant worms. To combat these feelings his first priority was to focus on the subjects that were essential to his education as a seminarian, and his scholarly discipline was reflected in his good grades. Although he tried hard to restrain his tongue—it had already gotten him into trouble at Colegio San José—his intellectual rebelliousness would not abate. Despite his best intentions not to draw attention to himself or to make enemies, he continued to pose questions that his teachers could not answer to his satisfaction.

For example, one day in theology class he asked,

"Where did Jesus say that women could not become priests? In the beginning of the church, St. Peter was married. That was the norm when the church was founded. When and why did the church hierarchy decide marriage was detrimental to the religious life?"

Whereas at Colegio San José he had been reprimanded for asking these kinds of questions, in Palos de la Quebrada his theology teacher responded, "Ignacio, maybe you'll be a famous theologian."

What Ignacio liked best about the seminary was that, for the first time in his life, he did not have to hide his homosexuality. There were cliques of openly gay novitiates. Shortly after his arrival he'd noticed that many priests and seminarians in Palos were coupled, and no one censored them. No one at the seminary was in danger of being expelled because of his sexual preference. Father Superior, he learned from Iván, regularly met in his office with the chief of police of Palos for trysts of his own.

Ignacio stopped feeling guilty for being sexually attracted to men. He came to the conclusion that Christianity had never dealt with the homoerotic conundrum at the heart of the story of Christ and His disciples. However, he decided to keep this conclusion to himself, even though the homoerotic—and sadomasochistic—implications of the image of Christ, half-naked and nailed to a cross, disturbed him. Ignacio decided not to share these thoughts with anyone, not even Iván.

After he'd arrived in Palos, Ignacio could not bring himself to write to Father Daniel because he was afraid of stirring his romantic feelings toward his former teacher. But now he was ready to contact him. Ignacio wrote a letter asking if he would be willing to engage in a correspondence about doubts that still troubled him.

Father Daniel replied by return mail: "I'm happy to hear from you. You can always write to me and I'll reply, if I can." In a second letter, in answer to Ignacio's questions about homosexuality and the church, he wrote back:

> I want you to know that the life I live in Colegio San José is no longer satisfactory to me. I haven't made a final decision yet about staying or leaving the organized church, but I will keep you posted about what I decide. In the meantime, I'm going to send you by separate mail a packet with some printed matter about a group of priests in Colombia who have joined the guerrillas to fight the government. After you read these materials, please destroy them. If they are found by the wrong people, you could get in trouble.

A fat envelope arrived two days later. Ignacio waited for his afternoon walk to open it. Before doing so, he pressed it against his chest, as if it still carried the warmth of Father Daniel's hands. Sitting under the gigantic ceiba tree near the village, Ignacio's heart raced as he read, and his hands trembled so much that the words went out of focus. He was doing something that his teachers would most likely not approve of and which could get him in trouble. Yet he was desperate to understand the position of the church regarding the genocidal conflict in the Putumayo. He read as quickly as he could because he didn't want to be late for dinner and arouse any suspicions.

In the bulky envelope were a few pamphlets about two Spanish priests who had come to Colombia inspired by Father Camilo Torres, who had been killed in combat with government troops in 1966. Ignacio was familiar with the name of this man, who had died when he was thirty-three. A teacher in Ignacio's mountain village school once mentioned that a priest named Camilo Torres had said, "Revolution is not only allowed but obligatory for all real Christians." Though he was eleven years old then, Ignacio became infatuated with the man who had uttered those unsettling words. Later, when he went to study in Facatativá, whenever a student mentioned Father Torres's name he was immediately forbidden to do so again. In the library at the *colegio*, Ignacio found a photograph of Camilo Torres in a book about 1960s Colombian history. Ignacio decided that when the day came that he had access to information that was not filtered through priests at the *colegio*, he would learn more about Torres. Yet the yellow mimeographed pamphlets from Father Daniel were not about Torres but about two Spanish priests, Fathers Domingo Laín and Manuel Pérez Martínez, who had come to Colombia from Spain. Father Pérez was known as El Cura *Pérez*. Upon his arrival in Colombia, Father Laín had been the parish priest of Meissen, one of the poorest barrios in Bogotá. He had found employment in a brickmaking factory in order to experience, as he explained in a newspaper interview, "in my own flesh, the exploitation and misery under which most Colombians live."

Ignacio decided the best way to hide the pamphlets, until he was ready to destroy them, was in plain view. He stuck them between some dusty Latin books on a shelf in the library. So desperate was he to read the rest of the packet's contents that he couldn't sleep that night. The following day, in Latin class, Ignacio was so distracted that the teacher asked him whether he was feeling well.

That afternoon, he read about Father Laín, and how he had joined a group of priests also interested in social justice, which had led to his being expelled from Colombia. In 1969, he'd slipped back into the country accompanied by Father Manuel Pérez. Among the pronouncements made by Father Laín, Ignacio liked one in particular referring to injustice in Colombia: "Once you know that situation, you cannot remain on the margins. You have to insert yourself in the fight against that situation if you really want to live in peace with your conscience." But the statement that made Ignacio shake, and which he read over and over, was, "You cannot flee. The world is full of hunger and poverty and you must bear witness to that reality."

Ignacio was mesmerized by the photos of Father Domingo Laín who, like Camilo Torres, was handsome and wore dark glasses. The pamphlets contained only the essentials of his life, and Ignacio was left with a hunger to know more about how Laín had died in a military skirmish with government forces in 1974, a few years before Ignacio was born. Ignacio was angry that he'd had to wait until he was in the seminary to learn about this. What else did he not know?

The next afternoon Ignacio read about Father Manuel Pérez, who for many years had been one of the leaders of the ELN guerrillas, an arm of which was still active in the Putumayo. Father Pérez had been excommunicated from the church in 1986 for involvement in the death of the Bishop of Araucas. Ignacio did not feel as drawn to Father Pérez as he had been to Father Laín: after all, Pérez was a man of war who had been involved in many bloody acts.

Ignacio wrote back to Father Daniel, thanking him for the clippings and articles. "I've read everything," he began. "Here we don't discuss politics; it's hard to know who's responsible for what. We have almost no news about what's happening in the rest of Colombia. Though the seminary is liberal when it comes to the life of homosexual priests in the church, we are discouraged from discussing national politics." Father Daniel had never said or done anything that would indicate he was gay, but Ignacio hoped that he would understand his need to talk about the feelings that tormented him. He added, "I think of you as my mentor, and what you believe about the life of the priesthood is important to me."

They kept corresponding with regular frequency, but Father Daniel never addressed at length Ignacio's questions about homosexuality. On the other hand, he did not discourage Ignacio from asking questions about the subject.

Ignacio mentioned Fathers Laín and Pérez to Iván on their next walk together. Iván halted, glancing behind them to make sure no one was within hearing distance, and said, "You're very young. At your age, in the village where I grew up, I didn't know anything about politics except what I heard on the radio. My teachers at school never criticized the government or the church—probably for fear of losing their jobs or getting killed by the paramilitaries. When my father and his miner friends got drunk in our backyard they cursed the Colombian government.

They were uneducated men, so I learned little about life outside our village." He frowned and shook his head. "For your own good, I advise you to keep your interests in the Spanish priests to yourself. Here in the Putumayo, people can get killed just for being curious. Wait till you leave the seminary; when you're far from here, you'll be able to learn about all that without risking your skin."

Father Daniel's next letter to Ignacio announced that he was leaving the religious life:

I'm not sure what I want to do next. What I do know is that I can't bear to stay in Colegio San José any longer, and I do not wish to be transferred to another Catholic school. While a part of me longs to become a man of action, another part wants to be a regular person in the outside world. As your friend, I pray that you will find the path that's best for you. I will not be writing to you again for a while. May God bless you.

With warm affection,
Daniel

The sudden end of their correspondence hurt Ignacio, but the pain was familiar to him. Though the circumstances were different, and it was now a few years since Lucas had ended their friendship so abruptly, the rejection still stung. Father Daniel, however, had been kinder—he had offered an explanation.

The seminarians in Palos did not get involved in political matters—they were influenced by the ideas of post–

Vatican II. Doing good works was known as a *charisma*. Pairs of seminarians were sent into the jungle, with a mission to help the Indians, who lived in isolated communities where there were no Catholic churches or schools. Despite the danger, the seminarians went with their rosaries as their only weapons. A seminarian who was one year away from graduating would be paired with a younger seminarian. Iván asked for permission to train Ignacio.

Sometimes they walked for days, on the open road or on paths that curled and dipped and rose in the sunless, insect-choked jungle. Sometimes they traveled by bus, or on the back of open trucks, or on rivers in tiny canoes that were often on the verge of toppling over, or flooding, or going under dark roaring currents, or even smashing against the massive rocks that appeared to have been placed there when the river was created.

In the villages deep in the jungle, they found sick and undernourished Indians who subsisted on the yucca and bananas they cultivated in tiny patches of soil carved out of the forest. Or they found what remained of a settlement: heaps of ashes indicating where huts had once stood. Strewn about were shards of clay vessels, and feathers and bones of animals the Indians had hunted.

"Look," Iván said at one of these ghost settlements, "the blackened bones you see scattered are of the people who were killed and burned." He sighed heavily. "It's obvious the rest left in a hurry and never returned to bury their dead."

Ignacio seethed with rage, but Iván was stoic, having seen this horrific tableau many times before.

After a while explanations were unnecessary: the

FARC, or the ELN, or the paramilitaries armed with powerful weapons—demanding their share of the trade of the coca plant and poppies—were responsible for the butchery. The people Ignacio and Iván saw walking the open roads that led to the cities were the survivors. "The lucky ones," Iván remarked one day, "are those who fled deep into the jungle, where the white man's greed cannot follow them."

There were times when Iván and Ignacio returned to the seminary without having made contact with any native people. On these occasions, Ignacio was grateful for having been spared one more appalling sight.

After their year of missionary work together, Iván graduated from the seminary and left Palos to attend university in Medellín. Ignacio, who persisted in his habit of not socializing, was then as lonely as he had ever been. He had gotten used to Iván's company and couldn't have asked for a kinder teacher. He now had a desperate need for the company of another person who was kind to him and with whom he could share friendship. After seeing so much misery firsthand, it was hard to remain optimistic about the nature of man. But Ignacio knew that if he succumbed to despair he would have to leave the seminary.

He had written to his parents a couple of times a year, whenever guilt prompted him to do so. His parents had to ask his sisters to write for them, and their brief letters of reply were impersonal. His family began to seem like characters in a discolored, silent dream. He was aware that they would reject him if they knew how he felt about the church, about God, and, especially, if they knew about his homosexuality. One day he mourned to himself aloud, "There's no one in the world who cares whether I live or die."

Ignacio had asked himself whether he should follow the example of Father Daniel and leave the seminary to join a guerrilla group to fight against the government. But having seen the wreckage created by the war, becoming a guerrilla no longer impressed him as a noble ideal. Besides, he had to admit that the prospect of living in the jungle did not appeal to him. He was not interested in trading the life of the mind and learning for a life of fighting, always being on the run, and killing. What had shaken him most deeply was discovering that there were no good people in the war, that the guerrillas, as well as the government and the paramilitaries, were interested not in justice but in spilling blood and enriching themselves.

Ignacio threw himself deeper into his studies. In another year he would be able to go to university, perhaps in Bogotá, which had been his cherished dream. It would be then, when he had left the jungle behind for good, that he would truly know himself, and his real life's work would begin.

Father Daniel had said to Ignacio before he was sent to the Putumayo, "Perhaps you'll never have faith. But that's not an insurmountable problem for a priest, if you can still be of use to God." Sensing Ignacio's ambivalence, he had added, "Try to improve the lives of those who suffer, and you'll be rewarded when you see their transformation—even if it's short-lived. Any moment of grace we humans can achieve, that's the greatest blessing."

In the Putumayo, Ignacio finally understood the meaning of Father Daniel's words.

* * *

Then Lucas entered Ignacio's life again. In Facatativá, fear had made him repress his feelings for Lucas, but in the Putumayo he had learned that inside the church everything was permitted, and everything was forgiven, as long as it was handled with discretion. Ignacio ached to have physical contact with another man; but he hadn't acted on his desires yet because the wounds opened by Lucas's rejection were still painful. Besides, he thought of himself as unattractive because of his Indian looks. He was afraid to flirt with other men for fear of being rejected or ridiculed.

As soon as Ignacio laid eyes on Lucas, when he was introduced at dinner as the new seminarian in the community, he had to admit to himself that the whole time he had been in the Putumayo, Lucas had never been far from his thoughts. They sat across from each other at the table. When his eyes caught Lucas's, Ignacio smiled shyly, hoping his expression showed the happiness he felt to see him again. Lucas smiled back and waved almost imperceptibly, slightly lifting the hand that was resting on the table.

Lucas had grown into a young man. In Facatativá, Lucas had seemed almost unaware of his beauty. Now he had the air of someone who, despite his modesty, understood the effect his physical attributes and charming manners had on others. It was hard not to look at him. In a room with many gay men, Lucas's presence was causing a quiet disturbance. His presence electrified the atmosphere in the dining room. The tips of Ignacio's fingers ached to caress Lucas's copious and lustrous chestnut hair. He felt an urge to stroke Lucas's neck, lock his arms around him, press him firmly against his chest, press his lips on his friend's mouth. He felt alarmingly helpless and vulnerable, unable to escape the enchantment cast by Lucas's golden-brown pupils. Ignacio clasped his hands under the table to stop himself from reaching across the table to touch him.

When the meal was over and they got up from the table, Ignacio saw that though Lucas had grown taller, his movements still had the nimbleness of a dancer. Ignacio touched his own forehead and thought he had a low-burning fever.

Just as when they first met, Lucas looked at Ignacio unguardedly, as if he saw no reason to conceal his thoughts. Ignacio remembered how charming Lucas's halting speech was, as if he couldn't think too far ahead of what he was saying. He could listen so attentively, as if he understood the things Ignacio couldn't quite articulate. Ignacio wanted to undress and ravish him. The need to touch his skin was so powerful that when Ignacio went to bed that night, he couldn't sleep.

The next day during recess Ignacio saw Lucas in the yard talking to another seminarian. During the hours he'd lain awake, he had acknowledged that he still couldn't forgive Lucas completely for dropping him the way he had. With great apprehension, he approached his old friend. Lucas hurriedly broke off his conversation with the seminarian and rushed toward Ignacio. He ignored the hand Ignacio extended to him and hugged him hard. Ignacio's hands trembled when Lucas's moist lips brushed his cheek and the stubble on his chin pressed against Ignacio's forehead.

As he finally pulled away Lucas said, "I was hoping you'd still be in the Putumayo."

Ignacio tried to regain his composure. "Why are you here in Palos?" he asked. "It's considered a punishment to be sent to this place."

Lucas blushed. "The Father Superior in Facatativá fancied me, but I didn't want to be his boy. The repulsive toad." He shuddered and then gave a nervous laugh. "So here I am."

"Well, welcome," Ignacio said. He was still afraid of showing Lucas how happy he was to see him again.

"I thought you'd still be mad at me because I shunned you without giving you an explanation," Lucas said. "They told me that unless I ended our friendship, I'd be sent back to my mother."

From that moment on they walked together every day, immersed in conversation—just as they had done in the past. Suddenly, Ignacio wanted nothing more from life than to see Lucas every day and spend time alone with him. *Maybe we will end up living together, working in the same parish*, he often thought.

Since his arrival at Palos, Ignacio's sleep had been fitful. Even during lulls in the gunfire that punctuated the night hours, he couldn't expel from his mind the screams, the chilling pleas of "No! For the love of God! No!" Other nights, even the innocent barking of the village dogs was enough to keep him awake until sunrise. The Paleros claimed the dogs barked because they saw the souls of the dead roaming the streets of the hamlet, hoping to see their loved ones. Ignacio was not superstitious, so he wondered whether the dogs barked because there were guerrillas or paramilitaries nearby. He knew that just because he was living in a community of religious people it was no guarantee that the seminary would not be attacked. When he felt most scared, Ignacio prayed that if his death were imminent, he would pass in his sleep.

After the seminarian who'd slept in the bed next to Ignacio's left for university in Cali, Lucas quickly moved his things to that spot, and no one said anything. To have Lucas sleeping so close to him was both reassuring and perplexing. After the lights went out, and the noises quieted, Ignacio longed to cross the few inches separating their beds and crawl under the sheets with Lucas. He burned with the desire to hold his friend naked in his arms, kiss his lips, and enter him. It was routine that sex took place at night in the dormitory where all the seminarians slept. The steady stirring of beds, the muffled cries of pain or ecstasy, the pungent smells that burst forth in the middle of the night—like the sweetly rotten carnal smell jungle flowers release to lure insects—were proof of that. However, Ignacio did not want to make the first move for fear of rejection.

Ignacio and Lucas reverted to being best friends, as if there had been no break in time; they were alone every chance they got. In the Putumayo, no one seemed to disapprove of their intimacy. Ignacio sensed that the other students gossiped about them, and many seminarians and priests looked at Lucas with lust, and perhaps envy, yet their closeness was not frowned upon.

By this time, Ignacio was a veteran of going into the jungle to carry out the message to the Indian communities. He asked the Father Superior to allow him to mentor Lucas, and permission was given. So once a week, Lucas and Ignacio would leave the seminary at dawn and

spend two or three days on the road—sometimes longer, depending on the distance they had to travel, or the
conditions of the roads in the rainy season, or the safety
in the areas that were controlled by any of the groups
involved in the war. Ignacio knew that every time seminarians went to proselytize in the jungle, it could be the
last day of their lives, but he kept this knowledge from
Lucas at first. Ignacio's consolation was that if they were
kidnapped or killed, at least he would die accompanied
by the person he cared about most.

Sometimes they went to villages within walking distance of Palos. When they we were heading to more remote parts of the jungle, they'd travel some of the way
by bus; sometimes they'd go by canoe to isolated settlements on the shores of the Orito River, where there were
no schools or churches. When they traveled farther than
usual and got caught in torrential rains, they would spend
the night in an Indian village, where they were usually
welcomed and given a hut to sleep in. The following day,
they'd raise a palm roof on four poles. That space would
become their classroom, where they taught the indigenous people the ABCs. On return visits, when they had
gained the trust of the villagers, Ignacio and Lucas began
to teach them the catechism.

Late one afternoon, they were sitting under a tall ceiba
tree near the soccer field. There was nobody in their vicinity, so Ignacio thought the time was propitious to share
some of the things he had wanted to say for so long. But
he still hesitated because he had always felt unattractive
compared to Lucas and had used this as an excuse to
repress his sexual feelings. However, since Lucas's arrival
at the seminary in Palos they had talked about homo-

sexuality openly and the old fear that his friend could expose him was gone. Still, Ignacio wondered whether Lucas would think reciprocating his feeling was tantamount to betraying his love for Jesus.

His palms got clammy but he was determined to speak now. "You know," Ignacio began, "I . . ." but the words abandoned him.

Lucas grabbed his hand. It was almost cold. Lucas let go of it; and Ignacio kept quiet. Finally, with a twinge of exasperation, Lucas said, "I think I know what you're going to say. By now you should know that homosexuality is a nonissue for me. For a long time, I struggled mightily with my feelings for men, and prayed not to be gay. Then one day I told myself I had been made this way—which could only mean that God approved of me."

After this conversation, Ignacio's desire for Lucas became so overwhelming that in his classes he heard the voices of his teachers as if they were speaking to him from continents away, or in languages he could not comprehend. He would forget to sweep a floor that he was scheduled to clean, or he would sweep it twice in the same day. When he was saying the rosary in the company of other seminarians, he would often lose his place.

One night in an Indian village hut, Ignacio lay next to Lucas on their straw mat and told himself that if he didn't let go of his inhibitions he would go mad. He placed his hand on Lucas's shoulder, then immediately wanted to withdraw it. Ignacio's entire body froze; he stopped breathing.

Softly, Lucas said, "Leave your hand there. I like it." Then he turned to face Ignacio with a smile. Lucas stretched out his arm, slipped his hand under the band of Ignacio's underwear, and grabbed his hard cock. They clasped each other in a tight embrace, leaving no space between their sweating bodies. They kissed with open lips, with a hunger that Ignacio found almost frightening. As they kissed, their hands explored each other's faces, hair, the back of their necks, shoulders, cupping and clasping each other's buttocks, pulling gently on each other's testicles. Ignacio had never been with a man before, so he knew he didn't have AIDS. For fear of breaking the perfection of the moment, he didn't dare ask Lucas if he'd been with a man before. Lucas's tears fell on Ignacio's face.

"What is it?" Ignacio asked. "Should I stop?"

"I'm crying out of happiness," Lucas whispered. "I'm still a virgin." Then he added, "I wanted you to be the first man to penetrate me."

After they finished making love, they slept in each other's arms, sweating in the sticky jungle air, the semen they had spilled on each other acting as an adhesive between their bodies. Now and then, the buzzing of the mosquitoes outside the netting would awaken Ignacio, and he would find Lucas holding him, his chest pressed against his back, his nose so close to his ear that he could feel whenever Lucas took the faintest breath. His exhale smelled of sweet basil.

When Ignacio awoke in the morning, Lucas held Ignacio's lower lip with his own lips.

Ignacio pulled back gently. "Good morning, Lucas," he said, and with those words realized that a new, hitherto unknown life was beginning for him.

Lucas leaned forward and pressed his open lips on Ignacio's and did not remove them until Ignacio yielded and they made love again.

They left the Indian village as the sun was still rising, before the heat of the day baked the soil. They walked in silence for hours, crossing wooden bridges, passing by other Indian villages, stopping at a hut only to ask for a drink of water. At one point, they were alone on a solitary stretch of the road when Lucas brushed his shoulder against Ignacio and then grabbed his hand.

"What are you doing?" Ignacio snapped, pulling his hand away. "Are you crazy? Don't ever do that in public again. You know how much trouble we could get in if people saw us?"

Lucas reached out and grabbed his hand again, tightly this time, and refused to let go as they walked in silence on deserted paths the rest of the day.

Years later, Ignacio would remember the period when he and Lucas trekked from village to village as the happiest time in his life. Each new morning he awoke excited to be alive. As they hiked on the red-dust trails of the jungle, Lucas often held a rosary in his right hand. To Ignacio it seemed as if Lucas derived sensual pleasure from rubbing the worn-out spheres of cedar. From the constant handling, the beads had turned black and acquired a waxy, varnished glow. Lucas found the monotonous repetitions comforting, and Ignacio envied his simple faith. In less charitable moments he'd think that for Lucas praying replaced thinking. Praying seemed to free Lucas from the self-doubt Ignacio struggled with all the time. Lucas was not a tormented soul like he: instead, Lucas found joy in the simplest activities. As time passed, Ignacio began to wonder if that was what it meant to live in the light of grace.

On one of their treks, passing an opening on the side of the road, Lucas said, "It looks like nobody has gone down there in a long time." With his usual puppy-dog eagerness, he added, "Let's find out."

Lucas pushed aside a thicket of branches that obscured the path. He made enough room with his bare hands to forge ahead; apprehensive, Ignacio followed him. The narrow overgrown path became wilder and thicker as they proceeded. Ignacio was much less curious than Lucas when it came to exploring new places. Sometimes, during their travels in the jungle—after making sure there was no one coming in either direction—they would stop to kiss or hide behind a tree for oral sex. Lucas was not as shy as Ignacio when it came to initiating sex in the jungle.

Lucas kept forging ahead. The wild vegetation had almost completely reclaimed the trail, and daylight hardly reached the soil. Ignacio was about to tell Lucas they should go back. According to his calculations, they were still several hours from their destination, a village of Siona Indians, and the jungle was full of dangers at night. But Lucas was like a child looking for treasure. As Ignacio opened his mouth to protest, Lucas pushed aside a heavy branch concealing an opening, full of light, and an eerily quiet lagoon. No birds sang or flew over it; no butterflies whirled about; no monkeys hollered in the fruit trees. Even the ever-present blood-crazed insects seemed absent. The trees surrounding the lagoon were as still as if they were made of clay.

They arrived at a clearing on a sliver of sandy beach. The clear lagoon was fed by a waterfall that flowed over a rock higher than the top of the tallest tree. Lucas

screamed in delight, dumped his backpack, stripped naked, and dove into the still pool.

"Come in," he shouted as he surfaced. "It's refreshing."

"Are you crazy?" Ignacio yelled back. "There could
be snakes in there, or caymans. And it's full of leeches."

Lucas was already swimming away with powerful stokes. Ignacio was angry—Lucas knew he couldn't
swim. In the mountains where he grew up, there were no
lagoons or rivers—just streams that swelled and became
dangerous during the rainy season. The Barís only bathed
in those streams during the dry season, when they were
not deep enough for swimming.

Suddenly, seeing Lucas swimming naked, his perfectly shaped buttocks, the muscles of his shoulders and
his back gleaming in the sunlight, his shapely arms strik-
ing the surface of the water with confidence, Ignacio knew
that what he was most afraid of was not being unable to
swim, but of becoming a prisoner of his lust for Lucas.

Ignacio sat on the burning sand, feeling dizzy. He was
relieved not to see the nasty red ants that tore at one's
flesh. As he closed his eyes, his head on his raised knees,
he had a sensation of déjà vu: he knew *that* lagoon; he
knew its shape—*it* was the image that had haunted his
dreams since he was ten years old. This was the lagoon
where the FARC had massacred the forty-eight boys.
Ignacio started to shake, afraid to open his eyes, terrified that he'd see the lagoon covered with the bloated
rotten corpses of the children. "No wonder the trail was
so overgrown," he murmured to himself. It was a place
where something so horrible had happened that the people of the region had decided to let the jungle reclaim it.

Ignacio didn't believe in ghosts or spirits of the forest as his parents did. But suddenly he felt suffocated by a powerful force trying to crush his lungs. His heart pumped so loudly he jumped to his feet. He took a step and stumbled toward the water. He heard Lucas call, "Are you okay?" Ignacio turned around, and ran from the lagoon as fast as his shaking legs would permit. He heard Lucas shouting after him. Eventually, he heard nothing but the sound of his own galloping heart and his feet breaking twigs as they hit the ground.

Ignacio finally reached the road, where he collapsed, gasping. He lay on his back on the open path, paralyzed. His eyes were the only part of his body that moved. Ignacio had had dreams in which he saw himself in a coffin, and everyone around him thought he was dead, and he wanted to open his eyes and scream, but couldn't.

Lucas arrived panting, half-dressed, soaked. He dropped their backpacks on the road, kneeled down, and gently cradled Ignacio's head on his lap. "What's the matter? Are you all right?" he asked. Lucas looked around frantically; nobody was coming in their direction.

At that moment, Ignacio saw how much Lucas loved him. Slowly, Ignacio began to feel a tingling in his arms, and in his legs, and with great effort he was able to move his head from side to side, gingerly. *I'm alive*, he thought. But he still couldn't speak.

Gently, Lucas kissed his forehead over and over. "You scared me so much. What happened back there, Ignacio?"

How could he begin to explain? He mumbled, "I'll tell you later . . . Let's go."

Lucas helped him to his feet. Ignacio broke into a fast walk, dragging his backpack in the red dust. Lucas ran after him, wrapped his arms around him to make him stop, and said, almost with desperation, "I love you, Ignacio. Trust me. I love you."

Ignacio turned around to face him, and wept on Lucas's shoulder.

In the weeks and months that followed their admission of love for each other, Ignacio felt as if a slab of granite in his chest had been removed; he felt less alone, and there were moments when, thinking about Lucas and dreaming about a relationship he.hoped would last for the rest of their lives, he experienced a joy and peace entirely new to him. Ignacio was still tormented because, unlike Lucas, he couldn't turn his love into something spiritual. What he felt for Lucas was carnal, of the flesh, telluric.

Ignacio had always despised those seminarians who chose the religious life because they could not face being openly homosexual in the world. He did not want to end up hating himself because his life was a hypocritical lie. Yet he had no choice but to ask for guidance from the God he didn't believe in. *Just send me a sign*, he implored, wondering all the time whether God could even hear him. The answer never came; or, if it came, he never knew.

It was no secret that Father Humberto, his confessor, was in love with a seminarian, so Ignacio decided to discuss his feelings for Lucas during his weekly confession.

"I'm glad you're being honest with me," Father Humberto said, without a hint of disapproval in his voice. "As you know, if we omit confessing the truth, we're still lying." He paused. "Ignacio, I don't believe it's a sin to be a priest and to love a man. The two things are not incompatible. What you have to be clear about always is that you cannot let your love for a man replace your love for

Jesus Christ. Our love for our Lord should always come first. All the other loves are of a lesser order. As long as you do that, there's no reason for you not to become a good priest."

Even after this conversation, Ignacio wasn't completely reassured. If he was too cowardly to do anything else but become a priest, then he wanted to make sure that he could at least have a useful life. He told himself that there had to be more he could do besides teaching the Indians to read and converting them to Christianity. He rehashed his discussions with Father Daniel at school in Facatativá about liberation theology. Father Daniel had said, "The poor need medicine, running water, schools, food, more than they need to learn the Gospels." Ignacio had seen the people of the Putumayo malnourished, ravaged by disease, massacred by the army and the guerrillas, and he was ashamed to admit that the seminary was not doing much to relieve their misery. "We can't talk to people just about their souls and forget that they live in their bodies," Father Daniel had told him. These words continued to ring in Ignacio's ears.

After four years in the seminary, Ignacio's and Lucas's training was coming to an end. In those years, life in Palos had become increasingly dangerous. Violence had escalated and no one was safe. The situation was aggravated when two men from the village came to the seminary for sanctuary. The FARC demanded that Father Superior turn the two men over to them. The guerrillas gave him twenty-four hours before they would storm the seminary and take them by force. That night the two men managed to leave the compound undetected and disappeared into the dark jungle. No one heard from them again. But that was not the end of it: the men's children were taken by the FARC and their wives and daughters were raped.

A few months after this incident, two seminarians disappeared in the jungle while they were evangelizing. No one claimed responsibility. Leaving the seminary, even to go into town, became unsafe.

Ignacio recognized that for the forces fighting in this war, both Indians and peasants were expendable because there was a seemingly endless supply of them. The peasants were inconvenient pests who stood in the way of the guerrillas, the paramilitaries, and the narco-traffickers who wanted control over the cocaine and heroin trade. It was as if the fertility of the land, its rich mineral resources, the variety of the fauna, were not a blessing to the people of the Putumayo, but a curse.

Ignacio had talked to Lucas about leaving the seminary before he finished his education and entering university, joining the thousands of villagers who were abandoning their plots of land to move to the cities. Lucas didn't like the idea, so Ignacio decided to stay. He would not leave without Lucas.

Then Lucas and Ignacio received word that they had both been awarded scholarships to Javeriana University in Bogotá. There they would spend the next three years studying theology and preparing to be ordained.

Ignacio was eager to be ordained and devote himself to helping the kind of people Jesus Christ had cared about. He still had doubts about the God they were taught to believe in, but he hoped that, as a priest, he could make a difference in the lives of others. Having Lucas go with him as he entered this new phase of their life was reassuring. By this time, Ignacio had come to think of Lucas as his partner for life. He couldn't imagine life without him.

He left the seminary in Palos de la Quebrada still troubled because he could not emulate Lucas's simplicity in believing in the existence or goodness of God. But as he was getting ready to say his goodbyes to the Putumayo, he took time to slow down and revel in the beauty of this place where he had found his mission in life—and love. He contemplated the irrepressible way everything in nature grew and continuously renewed itself, witnessed the mighty currents of the rivers sweep away anything in their path, and he concluded that only an all-powerful God could have created such relentless energy, beauty, chaos, and terror, and have all of them coexist. Nature by itself could not have been capable of creating it; nature, he had come to believe, thrived on anarchy. But as he stood under the immense ceiba trees to say goodbye to them, the trees of life, as the natives called them, seemed as durable and powerful as marble columns in an ancient Mesopotamian city. He observed how at their top the ceibas fanned out into a vast green cup that served as a nursery and sheltered so many disparate creatures, providing fruit for the indigenous people as well as the monkeys and birds the Indians ate, and the bees that produced the honey with which they sweetened their brews and their harsh lives. Ignacio marveled once more at the dazzling kaleidoscopic bands of brilliant macaws and parrots, which used the trees as rest stations, gathering to feed and exchange news of the jungle, to gossip joyously.

Ignacio noticed simple phenomena for the last time—how the clouds, for example, blew in one direction and the rivers flowed in the opposite. He thus concluded that natural selection by itself could not have created such an organizing principle and perfected such a sense of equilibrium; it became clear to him that nature itself had no interest in humanity. This led to his next conclusion: that the God who had created life was neither good nor bad, but more like an insatiably curious scientist who, drunk on his infinite inventiveness, loved to try out all of his ideas on his creations, including the human species, just to see what would happen. So, natural disasters, beastly creatures, the cruelty of man, awesome beauty, and abundance—all these things just happened of their own volition, once God had set the whole machinery in motion.

After so many years of studying and living the so-called religious life, the best Ignacio could come up with by way of explaining everything that distressed and frightened him was to admit how helpless people are to control the powerful forces unleashed by nature. Humanity had had no recourse but to invent the idea of God to justify the seeming futility of human endeavor, especially when humans tried, fruitlessly, to peer into the mystery of what happened after the flesh rotted and went back to become part of the earth. So human beings took the next step forward and imagined an afterlife where things made sense; they invented religions so they could convince themselves that God had indeed sent His only son as a sign that He felt remorseful for the fragility of the people and the world He had created. It was therefore up to humans to give hope to others who were suffering, to help them in whichever small ways they could, if for no other reason than that all of God's creations needed to be cared for and longed to be consoled. The priesthood, Ignacio told himself, was as good a way as any to help assuage the pain of life.

Ignacio left Palos convinced that no matter how hard he tried, he could never believe in God. But maybe, just maybe, regardless of his beliefs or lack of them, he could help those who needed the idea of a God, guiding and encouraging them as they searched for Him.

CHAPTER FOUR
BOGOTÁ
1998

IGNACIO CONFIDED IN LUCAS THAT HE WORRIED his classmates would be arrogant and look down on him because of his Indian looks and his unsophisticated manners.

"This is a fantastic chance for you to pursue your intellectual interests," Lucas answered. "Maybe the other students won't be as snooty as you think."

Ignacio wished he'd been born an optimist like Lucas, who believed that all you had to do was place your faith in Jesus Christ and then everything would turn out fine. Lucas had lived in Bogotá for a few years, but Ignacio had gone straight from the mountains of Norte de Santander to the school in Facatativá, and then to the seminary in the Putumayo. He was embarrassed about his limited knowledge of the world. For generations, people in his family had never wandered far from their place of birth. Bogotá was vast, like he imagined the sea to be—which neither he nor anyone in his family had ever seen. He found it hard to believe that something so immense really existed. To Ignacio, *bogotanos* seemed almost like beings from another planet.

Lucas tried to reassure him. "Don't worry, I'll be your Lazarillo and explain the people to you."

* * *

The university was located in a bustling part of the city, yet there were many aggressive beggars just across the street from the campus. On the mountain behind the campus a sprawling scatter of dwellings spread in all directions like gigantic tentacles assembled from scraps of wood, cardboard, bricks, and planks made of disparate metals. This neighborhood stretched almost all the way to the top of the mountain, and it was often buried under the clouds. During orientation week the new students were warned not to hike up the mountain by themselves, or even in small groups, because the place crawled with many displaced, lawless people. They built improvised homes wherever they found a plot of land; in the rainy season, flash floods swept away the flimsy houses or buried them under mudslides. The streams that descended from the mountain to the city below were a constant flow of sewage that often included animal and human carcasses. To Ignacio, Bogotá seemed like a city about to run out of land, and as brutal in its own way as the Putumayo. What reconciled him to the metropolis was that he had fallen in love with the green mountains surrounding it to the east, and he decided before long to check out as much of the city as possible.

Ignacio disliked the noisy streets and avenues clogged with buses and trucks that spewed nauseating black plumes. In Bogotá, as in the Putumayo, no one could relax—dangers lurked everywhere. The school had warned those students new to the city that while cars and buses waited at traffic lights, the passengers were often robbed—sometimes at gunpoint. The main difference between the city and the jungle was that in Bogotá, Ignacio could not easily identify the dangers.

He was painfully aware of being a peasant just arrived at the bus station. He asked Lucas to buy his clothes for him, so he would blend in more.

In the Putumayo, there had been two kinds of people, the peasants and the armed people, so he always knew whom he was dealing with. In the city, there were many other kinds of people whose professions or intentions he could not decipher. But his determination to get the most out of his education kept him going. He was keenly aware that it was his inquisitive mind that gave him an edge over his classmates. It was thrilling to have access to libraries that contained so many books he'd only heard about. Frequently, he was the last one to leave the library at night—he preferred being there than inside a church.

He wished he were like Lucas: handsome, friendly, and good-natured; anyone who came in contact with Lucas instantly liked him. He clung to Lucas like a child to his older brother. Another disadvantage was that Ignacio found it hard to mask how he felt about people. As had always been the case, he aced the academic part without the slightest trouble: he read the textbooks, did well on the tests, and accepted classes as part of the daily routine—something as routine as taking a shower, or brushing his teeth. He was surprised to find that he had no problem with praying; he enjoyed the periods of quiet and meditation.

Only a couple of his professors had interesting things to say; the rest taught as if they had memorized the textbooks and regurgitated ideas that no longer meant anything to them. It irked him that most students learned everything they were taught with an unquestioning mind. The majority of his classmates were passionate about playing soccer and going to soccer games, to mindless movies, and wearing the latest designer shoes and jackets. They seemed almost exclusively interested in how they looked, and their good manners and excessive politeness served only to hide their apathetic natures.

One afternoon he said to Lucas, "I get the impression that for them studying for the priesthood is just a more intellectual version of going to beauty school."

Lucas laughed. "You have a wicked tongue, Ignacio."

It bothered Ignacio that his tongue dripped poison, and he recognized this behavior as one of his major character defects. It was hard to restrain his critical streak, even though he knew that his harshness turned people away. But as long as he and Lucas were close, he thought, he'd be okay.

When he was feeling charitable, Ignacio could forgive his classmates their banal concerns, but what he couldn't forgive was that they seemed inured to the extremes of poverty and the hungry people visible everywhere. In the countryside people could at least always find some wild fruit in season when they were famished.

"What do you expect?" Lucas would say. "Most of these kids come from privileged families; the poor are another race to them."

Ignacio was no longer interested in being a contemplative poet-priest, like those who lived with Ernesto Cardenal in Solentiname. The Jesus Christ that appealed to him was the one who had used the lash to kick out the merchants from the temple. Around this time, he became obsessed once again with the story of the revolutionary priest Camilo Torres. Lucas gave Ignacio looks of concern when he started to quote Torres.

"Keep your enthusiasm to yourself," Lucas advised him. "Torres is persona non grata in the church nowadays."

Ignacio hated this cowardly side of Lucas; but in the infrequent occasions when he looked more charitably at life, he wished he had Lucas's practical nature.

On some afternoons when they had free time, Ignacio enlisted Lucas to accompany him by bus to the vast poor neighborhoods in the south of the city. Public transportation barely reached these places. Sometimes they'd get off the bus and wander around for hours.

"I don't see what's so fascinating about this," Lucas would complain. "These slums remind me of where I grew up. I can tell you anything you want to know about these shantytowns."

The miserable villages they explored had no hospitals, no schools, no sanitation, no running water. They were unregulated places where young men with guns stuck under their belts were the law.

"Don't make eye contact with them," Lucas often reminded him on their walks. "If we pretend we don't see them, they might not object to our presence."

Ignacio decided that after he was ordained, he'd ask to have his first parish in one of those neighborhoods. The rich would not be his flock. He already knew that what was most difficult for him was the pastoral part, the apostolate. So the focus of his priesthood would be what came hardest for him. He realized that in the years he had spent in the Putumayo teaching in the Indian communities, the results of pastoral work were palpable. Unlike the vague results of faith, he had proof that if you tried to improve the lives of others, you could see their transformation, even if it was short-lived.

He found relief by immersing himself in the textbooks. When it came time to choose a field of specialization, Father Guillermo, his advisor and part of the generation that had started liberation theology, said to him, "You're an excellent student, brother Ignacio, but I don't think you're a scholar. You're more interested in social causes, in action, than in theology. We need more young priests like you in the church. I'd suggest that you consider specializing in bioethics. It might be a good fit for you."

Ignacio had heard about this field of study but wasn't sure what it was.

"Look," Father Guillermo told him, "the conservative elements of the clergy think bioethics are all about cloning embryos; and they think of it as a modern kind of witchcraft. Those are the same priests who think any talk of evolution or DNA is heresy. They oppose the use of experimental vaccines in healthy people to find cures for illnesses about which we know very little. But I believe that like me you'll end up thinking about bioethics as a science that sees human beings as subjects worthy of investigation. In other words, first and foremost, bioethics says that each one of us is accountable to ourselves for our own acts, and that we cannot delegate our moral responsibility to anyone else."

Ignacio was so excited by this explanation that he decided his path right then. "Father, I'm very interested," he said enthusiastically.

When he told Lucas about his decision to study bioethics, his friend's response was, "Maybe I should study the same."

Ignacio was irked at the facility with which Lucas could make such an important choice. "It has to be a personal decision," he snapped, even though he sensed that Lucas was simply trying to make sure they remained as close as possible.

Lucas blushed and lowered his gaze. "You mean that I'm less interested in helping the vulnerable than you are."

Ignacio was moved by these words. They had been lovers now for almost four years, yet this awkward moment was the closest they had come to acknowledging that they wanted to be together for the rest of their lives.

"I know you're interested," Ignacio said. "I'm sorry I said what I said."

From then on, under Father Guillermo's guidance, Ignacio and Lucas immersed themselves in the study of pluralistic ideologies. Being in the same field of study gave them a legitimate reason to spend more time together.

The students lived in the dormitories, where each had his own room; however, they were discouraged from spending time alone with their classmates in their rooms. The seminarians who had families in Bogotá could go visit them on weekends, so Lucas would often visit his mother in Suba, and he invited Ignacio to come along.

Lucas was proud of his mother's success in the world. Clemencia was such a good employee that she had been promoted to manager. The first time the two of them visited, she gave Ignacio her bedroom and slept on the couch in the living room. But when Ignacio returned for his next visit, he found that an extra bed had been placed in Lucas's room. For the first time ever, they could sleep together in their own room, and they could make love without fear of being caught. They tried hard not to make too much noise. It wasn't easy—Lucas was very vocal while making love. In the mornings, Clemencia behaved as if she hadn't heard anything the night before. When Ignacio mentioned to his friend how shy he felt about the arrangement, Lucas winked. "She uses earplugs to sleep when we visit."

At first Ignacio felt uncomfortable during his weekend visits because there was a lingering sadness about Lucas's mother that she clearly couldn't shake off. When he remarked on this, Lucas explained that his mother was heartbroken because she had not been able to get her two daughters to join her in the city. Lercy, the oldest, had married and moved with her husband to Neiva, hours away from Bogotá.

"When my mother got in touch with her," Lucas added, "Lercy wrote back to say that she could never forgive her for leaving them behind with Father."

One morning while Lucas was off shopping at the market, Clemencia joined Ignacio in the kitchen as he was having his breakfast. She poured herself a black coffee and sat at the table across from him. She smiled; the two had never found themselves alone. Ignacio started to feel fidgety and wanted to get up and run away.

She finally broke the silence: "After Lucas left the farm, I was very sad that he didn't have the companionship of his sisters. Though I've never regretted leaving his father, a part of me blamed myself for separating Lucas from his sisters. Long before I met you, Lucas mentioned you so often that I felt like I already knew you. You're the only close friend he's ever had. I want you to know that for me, you're a member of our family." She took a long sip of her coffee, as if to give him time to speak. "I like it black, without sugar or milk," she finally said.

Since Ignacio remained quiet, she went on: "I know your parents are far away and that nobody can replace them, but you can always think of me as a kind of substitute mother." Then she got up and gave him a hug. "Now, let me make you some scrambled eggs for breakfast. When you're here, you don't have to eat like a monk."

Ignacio understood that Clemencia had given her blessing to their relationship. A few years later, when she died of heart failure, he mourned for her almost as if she had been the mother he'd lost when his parents sent him to school in Facatativá.

After two years at Javeriana, Ignacio was not any closer to accepting that God—if He existed—cared about humanity. He had a hard time believing that Jesus was, as they were taught, inside every man. Or that God was to be found everywhere. What part of Jesus Christ was in the heart of murderers? And why did God allow the atrocities perpetrated everywhere? Was His role exclusively to witness? Or was God an accountant who kept tally of one's sins and decided who would be saved and who would burn in hell for eternity?

Despite his doubts, Ignacio still wanted to be a priest, but he was tormented by the fact that he didn't know if he was staying in the church simply because he was afraid to cast off the shield of the religious life. Or was he staying because the church gave him an excuse not to take responsibility and make choices? Ignacio had no answers to his questions, so he remained.

CHAPTER FIVE
SOACHA
2004

AFTER IGNACIO AND LUCAS WERE ORDAINED, they were assigned to two different parishes in Bogotá. Father Guillermo had advocated that Ignacio be assigned to Soacha, a neighborhood in the south of Bogotá, where some 400,000 displaced people had settled in the last decade, seeking refuge from the violence in the Colombian countryside. Although Ignacio sensed that many of his classmates saw his first assignment as a kind of penance, he was convinced that he was being sent to a place where he could do the kind of social work he'd always dreamed of doing.

Ignacio was shocked to find out that after his years at university he had forgotten the smells of poverty. From the beginning of his education in the church, one of the things he liked best about it was the burning of incense and myrrh during Mass, and the aromas of fresh flowers that always adorned the altars. The church, he felt, shielded him from the disagreeable smells of the world.

As a boy, he had detested the stench of dead animals in the countryside left to rot in the sun: dogs run over by vehicles, poisoned cats, and the horses or burros that died of incurable diseases, whose carcasses were left to wait for their winged undertakers—the black vultures he found so disgusting—to reduce them to a pile of bones.

As long as he could remember, Ignacio had made a point of avoiding smelly people, as if they had the plague. He had always been meticulous with his own personal hygiene, and was fastidious about germs. What he liked best about women was that many of them smelled nicer than men, as if they had just showered with a fragrant bar of soap. But as he went into the world to bring the message, he found that many of the people he worked with—the poor, the displaced, the disenfranchised—smelled terrible. Many of them had never used deodorant. He finally had to accept that he could not expect the poor he worked with to smell like his favorite scent of all—aromatic eucalyptus groves.

Los Altos de Cazucá, the barrio where Ignacio was to launch his first church, was located on the slopes of the mountains south of the city, nine or so miles above Soacha.

The archdiocese gave him a room in the parish in Soacha, and a small salary. Every morning Ignacio took a bus to Los Altos de Cazucá and then explored its grass-covered streets to introduce himself to the people.

He decided his first project would be to build a place where he could say Mass under a roof. In Bogotá, where it rained often and drizzled almost nonstop, this was essential. He couldn't ask for donations from people who survived mostly on boiled potatoes. Very soon Ignacio discovered that he had no option but to succeed. For a nonbeliever, he told himself, this might be a way to understand faith.

He chose a spot of grassy land on a promontory that

no one had built on, maybe because the terrain at the top of the knoll was uneven. He decided he would start by leveling the ground. So he went from door to door asking for volunteers to help him raise a wooden structure on that piece of land, where he could deliver Mass and live in a one-room rectory. People received him respectfully, and many of them invited him in for a cup of coffee. One old woman said, "Father, I prayed every day that God would send somebody to help us. The gangs rule this place; the only law they obey is the gun."

Most people looked at him with skepticism. Their attitude seemed to be, *Besides saying Mass and baptizing children, what else can the church do for us?*

He started showing up every morning around seven o'clock carrying a shovel and rake. He spent many hours of the day removing—a patch at a time—the carpet of grass that covered the ground. Then he raked the soil to clear it of roots and pebbles. Soon, women showed up with cups of hot coffee and sometimes a roll. Or they would send their children with pots filled with water and a drinking cup. Ignacio felt encouraged by these signs. One morning a boy came around noon and said, "Father, my mother sends you this soup and rice."

Ignacio felt bad taking food from these people who had so little, but he understood that these humble offerings meant they accepted him. He stopped working to receive the food and sat on the ground to eat. The boy sat too and waited for Ignacio to finish eating. Ignacio tried to engage him in conversation, but the boy was shy. Ignacio managed to get out of him that his name was Norberto. When he had finished the food and returned the kitchenware, Ignacio said, "Tell your mother the food was delicious. May God bless her for her kindness." The boy smiled, got up, and left quickly without saying a word. "Please tell your mother I'm very grateful to her," he called after the boy, who ran in a great hurry down the slope. When he got to the bottom of the hill, he turned back, waved at Ignacio, and finally smiled.

Ignacio sensed that he was being tested. And as time went on, more children and elderly women would stop by to chat or to bring him something to eat. Among them was Señora Graciela, a plump middle-aged woman who carried her extra weight like a bouncing wraparound ornament hugging her body. She spoke loudly, as if she were used to giving orders to unruly children. But she smiled all the time, and broke into raucous laughter when Ignacio least expected it. Señora Graciela owned the corner store at the bottom of the slope. "You know, Father, you don't have to carry your shovel and rake every day from Soacha," she told him the second time she stopped by. "You can leave them in my store overnight. I'll take good care of them for you."

Señora Graciela's visits had the effect of a high-ranking official blessing Ignacio's project. Days after her second visit, two older men came by and introduced themselves as unemployed construction workers. They offered to help him with the project until they found work. One of the men, Señor Hugo, brought a wheelbarrow. With their help, things progressed quickly and soon they had cleared the ground and were ready to start laying the foundation.

Ignacio had never built anything in his life, but with the help of Señor Hugo and Señor Aristides, he drew a plan for a simple structure. Pleased with Ignacio's efforts, the archdioceses of Soacha and Ciudad Bolívar provided funds to buy wood, tools, and building materials. People began to bring him unused planks they had in their homes, along with nails, wire, bricks, and glass. On weekends, boys and girls started coming by with their parents, and sometimes their teachers, to give a hand.

Los Altos de Cazucá was so violent that even the police shunned it: the barrio was run by warring gangs that killed anybody who opposed them. Before long, the thugs began to take an interest in what Ignacio was doing. They would gather below the mound and watch Ignacio and his volunteers for hours, smoking and making rude comments. Regularly, they pulled out their guns and flashed them, as a reminder of who was in charge. Ignacio worked in silence around them. Sometimes he'd wave at them, but they never waved back. Now and then one of them would mumble something or nod brusquely in his direction.

Four months after he arrived at Los Altos de Cazucá, Ignacio moved into the parish house and delivered his first Mass. He began his ministry full of optimism, committed to preaching God's word in a personal way: going to visit the sick and those too old to leave their homes, taking the message from person to person. Though the days of liberation theology were long in the past, he discovered a few post–Vatican II priests in Bogotá who were devoted to easing the harsh lives of the people struggling on the fringes of the great metropolis.

Ignacio and Lucas saw each other at least once a week, and the two men spoke on the phone often during the day. Every morning before he started his workday, Lucas would call to say, "Good morning, Ignacio." And every night before he went to sleep, he'd call to wish Ignacio a good night.

Most Sundays after the noon Mass, Ignacio traveled half an hour by bus to Barrio Kennedy to stay overnight with Lucas. This was usually the only time during the week that they could be alone together. Those Sunday nights were the great pleasures of Ignacio's life. Barrio Kennedy was much more prosperous than Soacha; Lucas's parish house had comforts that Ignacio's lacked. The two men would drink a bottle of wine with dinner, prepared by Lucas's cook, and then watch a movie. Though Ignacio didn't share Lucas's taste in movies (Lucas loved Hollywood spectaculars of Old Testament stories, Technicolor epics about the persecution of Christians during Roman times, and action blockbusters with Sylvester Stallone), he never complained. After the movie was over, they would retire to Lucas's comfortable king-size bed with soft sheets, cotton blankets, and feather pillows. Although Ignacio often felt guilty that there were so many in Bogotá who slept outside during the chilly nights, he had to admit that he enjoyed the relative luxury in which Lucas lived.

The days when Lucas and he made love feverishly were now in the past, but they hadn't yet grown indifferent to each other's bodies, and their tenderness had survived. Ignacio still loved Lucas's supple figure and hairless skin and he relished holding him throughout the night, and waking up in each other's arms.

Lucas seemed less interested in sex than Ignacio, but Ignacio was certain that he was not having sex with other men. Though more and more people in Bogotá were dying of AIDS, and everyone was aware of the disease, the two men continued to have unprotected sex. The days were over when Colombians believed that AIDS was a disease that only "gringos" got. In Soacha, Ignacio had seen many men, and some women, who were obviously sick. They were shunned, and often ostracized, by people in the barrio, and frequently by their own families.

One night after they had made love, Ignacio mentioned to Lucas that he was troubled by how poorly people with AIDS were treated. "I would like to try to do something about it. Even if it's just in Soacha."

Lucas remained quiet, as if he were mulling over Ignacio's words. Finally he said, "If I were you, I wouldn't count on the support of the bishop." Then he leaned over, kissed Ignacio on the cheek, and fell asleep.

Ignacio tried to find allies among the priests he met, but it made him sick to his stomach to find out that many of them were inordinately interested in driving their nice cars, getting expensive haircuts, buying jeans and sneakers by famous designers, owning the latest computers and cell phones, and traveling abroad. Their eyes shone more brightly when they spoke about these things than when they spoke about doing anything for their parishioners. Getting promotions and being transferred to churches in prosperous neighborhoods were the top priorities. More than ever, Ignacio was convinced that a message of a dignified life on earth was what Jesus Christ had wanted for his followers.

When he attended church congresses and celebrations, Ignacio resented seeing the cardinals and archbishops dressed in magnificent gowns and headdresses with gold threads. *With what they paid for those osten-*

tatious headdresses, thousands of people could be fed for months, he would think to himself.

One day, in a bout of anger, he complained to Lucas, "How did Jesus Christ's message get twisted like that? What do these pompous and vain men who lead the church have in common with a barefoot Jesus Christ and the humble carpenters, fishermen, and farmers who followed him, who trekked the roads of Galilee, slept in the open fields, under trees, in caves, without material possessions?"

"If you want to help the people," Lucas replied softly— the way he spoke when Ignacio was upset—"keep your views to yourself. By now you should know that in the church, if you want doors to open, you have to act and speak with humility. Otherwise you'll be ostracized. Worse, you may be transferred to the countryside—for the rest of your life."

Eventually, it was not enough for Ignacio to say Mass and to hear people's confessions. He decided to open soup kitchens in Los Altos de Cazucá and Soacha. First, he approached the archdiocese of Bogotá, realizing that without an important member of the church hierarchy in his corner, he wasn't going to get the help he sought. The archdiocese answered that at the moment they were overwhelmed with the social programs they had started in the last decade. In his usual conciliatory manner, Lucas advised Ignacio not to be blinded with anger and resentment, and to look elsewhere for allies. Ignacio had heard about a community of Sisters of Charity of the Incarnate Word. On the grounds of their convent, they had built a residence for elderly homeless people. These nuns had extensive orchards where they cultivated fruit, vegetables, and flowers for the needs of the convent. But they were such good gardeners that they produced a lot more than they needed, and they donated the extra produce to food pantries.

The convent was located on the outskirts of the town of Villetas, less than an hour away from Soacha. Ignacio took a bus to Villetas and got off at the main plaza. Asking for directions, he made his way to the convent. Ignacio explained to the nun who guarded the door that he was there to see the Mother Superior.

"Follow this path, Father, and you'll find Mother Angela in the vegetable garden." She pointed to a brick path that disappeared amid the shrubbery.

It was a sunny morning, and the colors in the orchard made him dizzy. It was refreshing to be far away from Bogotá and surrounded by greenery. Ignacio found Mother Superior collecting ripe tomatoes and putting them in a basket on her arm. Each tomato that she plucked, she brought to her nose and inhaled deeply. She was so absorbed in her task, Ignacio thought, that she could have been selecting emeralds. When she saw him approach, she stopped and smiled at him. Mother Angela stood erect and still as she waited for him. Ignacio had heard she was ninety-one years old. She was small, wiry, and her face was scored with deep wrinkles. Her head was uncovered. *She must have been a pretty girl once*, he thought, because there was still something beautiful about her face. Her large brown eyes held him rapt.

He introduced himself, and then said, "I've come to see you, Mother Angela, because I admire your social works very much and need your advice."

"Welcome," she replied, and shook his hand with a firmness that surprised him. She pulled out a pair of glasses from her apron pocket and put them on. "I don't use them to pick tomatoes or anything from the orchard. For that, my hands are better judges than my eyes. Now I can see you better. You are young. I like the energy of young people. Well, Brother Ignacio, I was about to return to the kitchen with these tomatoes. I get tired easily when it's hot, like today. Will you walk me?"

Ignacio offered to carry the basket, but she declined. After she dropped off the tomatoes on a long, scarred, wooden table, Mother Angela invited him to her office. There was a desk and chair for her and two chairs across from her. The furniture was unadorned. Her desk was spotless and free of clutter. From an aluminum thermos she poured two cups of a very aromatic tea. There were green leaves in the liquid she filled the cups with. He took a sip.

"It's mint from our garden," she told him.

He sipped the brew and hummed with pleasure, which made her smile. There was a small wooden cross on one side of the room, and opposite it, a small statue of the Virgin Mary on a pedestal. Light poured in from a window behind Mother Angela. The branches of a tangerine tree heavy with fruit pressed themselves against the windowpanes.

She asked him to tell her a little about himself. When Ignacio spoke about what he had been doing in Los Altos de Cazucá she leaned forward on her desk, holding her tea mug in both hands. "May God bless you for your charitable heart," she said when he had finished. "I'm so pleased to meet you. Young people like you are the future of the church." She paused. "What can I tell you about us that will be useful to you in your work? Some years back, a small number of the younger sisters were dissatisfied that we spent our lives praying, locked up behind these convent walls, even though we had the example of Mother Teresa of Calcutta. This led to a reexamination of what the monastic life meant. We are not a wealthy community, but we are rich in land. And we weren't putting it to good use. From the time the convent was founded, we've kept orchards that provide us with most of the food we eat. About twenty years ago, it became impossible to ignore the many displaced people who knocked on our doors every day asking for something to eat. That's when we decided to use the land to grow food to feed the hungry. Visitors to the convent often remarked about the beauty of the roses we grow here. That's when we began to plant more rosebushes to sell the flowers in the city. With the money that started coming in, a place for homeless old people was built on our grounds." Noticing that Ignacio had barely touched his tea, she asked, "May I offer you something else to drink?"

Embarrassed, he shook his head. "It's delicious, Mother. It's just that I was so engrossed in your story." He took a long sip.

"I'll give you a bunch of fresh leaves to take back to the city," she said before continuing. "Well, Brother Ignacio, the more vegetables and fruit we grew and gave away, the more fertile the orchards became. It was as if Mother Nature herself were pleased with how we were putting her gifts to use. Though more hungry people started knocking on the doors of the convent to ask for whatever we could give away, we were still left with so much that we rented a truck. Fortunately, Sister Lucia of the Immaculate Conception knew how to drive a stick shift. So we began to deliver the excess fruit and vegetables to the most afflicted neighborhoods. It's as simple as that."

Soon after his visit to Villetas, the old priest in Soacha died, and Ignacio was transferred there. Brother José Luis, a young priest whom he liked, and who had recently been ordained, was named as his replacement in Los Altos de Cazucá. Ignacio was sad to say goodbye to the people of a neighborhood he had become fond of, but he was quick to see that from Soacha he could expand the influence of his ministry. In the last decade, its population of Soacha had grown by over a quarter of a million people who mostly lived in poverty, but they were prosperous compared to the people in Los Altos de Cazucá. There were entrepreneurs who had started little businesses; a few schools for children had been built in garages. The church in Soacha was as impressive as a cathedral by comparison with the wooden church building in Los Altos de Cazucá, and the parish house was new and comfortable. An office and a secretary came with the new assignment. Ignacio was pleased to discover that there was still plenty for him to do in Soacha to improve the living conditions of his parishioners.

Not too long after he settled into his new parish, Ignacio became aware that here, too, gangs terrorized the population. Whereas in Los Altos de Cazucá they had left him alone, in Soacha, during one of his first walks in the neighborhood, as he passed a group of angry-looking youths, they greeted him with catcalls. Ignacio ignored the provocation and kept walking until he heard someone yell, "Welcome to Soacha, Mother Teresa!"

Ignacio turned around. Then, without thinking about what he was going to do, and as if he felt protected by an impenetrable cloak, he marched in their direction, his face distorted in a scowl, his lips twisted in a grimace, his eyes glaring with anger, his fits clenched. Confronted with his rage, the startled thugs dispersed in different directions, laughing. The gang—which he soon found out called itself the Brotherhood of the Knife—didn't bother him again as he walked the streets of Soacha. However, he remained aware that this incident was just a taste of more unpleasant interactions to come. Later, he learned from his parishioners that the gang extorted money from business owners, supposedly to protect them from other gangs and the police. They demanded payments from Soachans for a "vaccine," the same kind of extortion tax the peasants and the Indians in the Putumayo paid to the cartels and the paramilitaries.

The gang members were a small band of brutes, but the displaced children he ran into on the streets of Soacha every day numbered in the thousands. The children reminded him of the rapacious schools of piranhas he had seen in the Putumayo's rivers attacking human flesh. Ignacio had wanted challenges as a priest, but he started to wonder whether he had the strength to deal with all of these evils. He knew he had to make a choice, so he opted to ignore the gangs for the time being and instead try to do something about the children.

Even before the transfer to his new parish, Ignacio had been aware of the displaced kids who streamed into

Bogotá from war zones. Most of them had lost both parents, and often their entire families. He had seen children
like these in the Putumayo, hungry, traumatized, traveling the roads, focused on finding something to eat and
getting far away from the massacres. In their trek to the
cities, these children often met others marching away
from the jungle and followed them. Along the way, they
robbed travelers, stores, gas stations, and raided the isolated farms of settlers for food, clothing, or anything they
could sell. It was routine to kill the people who offered
resistance. Like the marauding swarms of red ants in the
jungle that devoured everything they found on their path,
these desperate children left behind a trail of desolation.
Along the way, a deep anger swelled in their masses and
they committed acts of savagery, which were particularly
shocking because they were perpetrated by children. As
Ignacio watched them roam the streets of Soacha, stopping people to aggressively demand money or food, he
was struck by the blankness in their eyes, as if they had
no souls. If they were denied, they took, by force, whatever they wanted. People walking alone, or late at night,
had been mugged—and sometimes stabbed. As these displaced children roamed the streets, or gathered in empty
lots, you could hear them singing death songs of revenge
against the paramilitaries, the FARC, and the government. Ignacio shuddered at the thought that they seemed
like a grim army of demonic creatures.

Ignacio continued visiting Mother Angela every chance
he had. After each visit, he felt the heaviness in his heart
had been made lighter. One day she said to him, "Ignacio,
it's clear to me that you're on this earth not to baptize

the children of the rich, but to help the poor. I'm too old now to leave these walls where I've lived most of my life, to go live in a barrio where I'm truly needed. But I think this will be your mission and you must not postpone it. You will be unhappy unless you do what your heart is telling you to do. Otherwise, you'll end up hating the church. I believe you've already realized that to do something about injustice you have to risk the tranquility of your own life. It won't be easy. Colombian people are not charitable by nature. Because of the oppression in which we've lived, we have become cannibals of other Colombians. The hardships of our lives have made us envious—we are motivated by envy, so we compete with others out of envy; we kill out of envy; the happiness of others makes us miserable."

Ignacio was shaken by her words, and found he had no response; he was struck silent by her brutal honesty.

Mother Angela went on: "There won't be very many clergymen in the church who will want to help you. You'll need the strength that only faith can give you. I sense that you don't pray much, but I urge you to pray to God, even if you don't believe in Him or in the use of prayer. When I pray, I wrestle with the devil. It's that wrestling that has given me the strength to continue on the path I've chosen." She paused, but he remained quiet. "I sense that you come to see me looking for reassurances. The only thing I can tell you, my son, is that most people go through life seeking desperately for love. We want to be loved; we are miserable if we can't get the love we think we need. What I've learned is that we have to *earn* love. We have to learn to give love to others before we can receive God's love."

* * *

Ignacio had gotten into the habit every morning of going for coffee and a buttered roll at the bakery across the street from the church. He soon became friends with the owner, Doña Ana, who made her own bread, which she served him while it was still warm from the oven. Ignacio was also fond of the chicken and pork tamales she made for lunch. The people in the neighborhood stopped by her eatery to get their daily staples: rice, eggs, flour, lard, sugar, milk, and potatoes. She was a pillar of the community and he enjoyed her gossip about the people of Soacha.

Doña Ana was a widow who had raised four children by herself. She lived alone now in the back of the store. As they got to know each other, their discussions extended to social problems. She was fed up with the displaced children who came to the bakery to beg for food. Ignacio mentioned to her that he wanted to start a social program for the displaced of Soacha, with or without the help of the church.

One morning, after several children had stopped by aggressively begging for morsels from the customers, she exploded: "Father, you know I give them whatever I can afford to give him, but I can't feed all of them! I have to make a living. And they've become pests. They scare away my customers."

"I would like to do something," Ignacio said, "but my hands are tied. When I've mentioned our problems to my higher-ups in the archdiocese, they act as if they're deaf."

Doña Ana sighed. "Father, my children are grown up and have good jobs, thank God. I've saved 600,000 pesos and I will give them to you to get started, if that helps. As much as those children terrify me, they are creatures of

God too." Then she went back behind the counter to take care of a customer.

Ignacio was so astonished by her generosity that he left the store after he finished his coffee without thanking her. He was not superstitious, but even he had to admit that this was some sort of sign. Later that day, when he stopped by the drugstore to get some aspirin and toothpaste, he mentioned Doña Ana's offer to Don Augusto, the pharmacist. Maybe not to feel outdone by her, Don Augusto said, "I know you're not asking me for money, Father, but I can give you 300,000 pesos. I can do that much."

Ignacio was in a quandary about what to do with the money that suddenly had come his way, but he knew he had to put it to good use. When he spoke to Lucas on the phone, he mentioned what had happened and asked if he had any ideas about what he should do next.

"Pray and ask God to show you the way," Lucas replied.

The truth was that Ignacio had never prayed to God for anything for himself. *I should've known better*, he thought, and smiled. *Lucas believes prayer is the answer to everything.* He needed the advice of a practical-minded person; making money had never been one of his strengths.

He mentioned his dilemma to Doña Ana. "You need to grow that money," she said. "Let's do a raffle." She took a calculator from the pocket of her apron and began to press its keys. "If we sell a thousand tickets for five thousand pesos each, and the winning ticket gets 500,000," she kept pressing buttons, "we'll end up with 4.5 million pesos. That'll be enough to get started."

At Sunday noon Mass, Ignacio announced the amount of money that had been collected to help the displaced; he added that there would be a weekly raffle, and told the amount of the first prize. A murmur rose from the usually silent congregation and then people began to clap. At the end of the Mass, many parishioners approached to ask him if they could buy a ticket. At the first weekly raffle Ignacio sold over two thousand tickets.

Doña Ana, whose acute business entrepreneurship surprised Ignacio, suggested that they could also ask the parishioners to contribute valuable possessions they didn't need. A local businessman who owned a thriving brick factory donated a small plot of land, and within two months a simple brick structure was built. It consisted of a big room, a bathroom complete with shower stalls, and a kitchen. Other locals donated planks of wood, and volunteer carpenters worked on weekends building tables and chairs.

When the doors opened to offer a hot lunch to those who could not afford to feed themselves, over a dozen nuns sent by Mother Angela went to work in the food kitchen. After a few weeks, when the children realized they were not going to be captured and shipped off to government institutions, they began to show up for lunch every day. Soon, the food kitchen was feeding soup and rice to over two hundred children daily

On their own, the nuns began a campaign to collect old clothes and shoes that were still in good condition. The homeless children were encouraged to trade in their filthy rags for clothes that were washed and ironed.

A year later, a large new room was added to the structure; it became a classroom furnished with desks, chairs, and a blackboard. By the following year, a clinic was added. More nuns from Mother Angela's convent arrived, and they began to teach the children the basics of reading and writing.

Many of the children were intractable, addicted to sniffing glue, smoking crack cocaine and methamphetamine, and shooting heroin; they were used to stealing and mugging people to pay for their supply. A large number did not want help getting off these drugs, which they considered the only solace in a depressing life that seemed without a future. They knew that many of them would wind up in jails, or become prostitutes, eventually ending up with AIDS, or simply disappear, and nobody would miss them.

But a small number of them learned skills and, with guidance provided by the nuns and other religious people, found their way to the few government agencies that could help them apply to trade schools. It was easy to get discouraged. Ignacio realized that in most cases he was merely dressing a wound. However, now and then a boy or a girl escaped the vicious cycle and that became his main incentive.

When news spread about what the parish in Soacha was doing, volunteer doctors and nurses started arriving from other cities in Colombia. People even came from countries as far away as Canada, the United States, Germany, France, Spain, and Cuba. The volunteers brought with them medical equipment and much-needed medications.

One day Ignacio realized that what had started as a small project to feed hungry displaced children had grown into a full-time job.

Ignacio and the nuns had kept the center running without the help of the church. But as the social work in Soacha became an object of increasing media attention, Archbishop Piedrahita contacted him. "I'd like to come and see what you're doing, Brother Ignacio."

Ignacio obsessed about the visit. Should he paint the room? Buy new chairs and desks for the classroom? What should he serve Archbishop Piedrahita? Finally, he decided not to try to dress up anything.

After the tour of the place, the archbishop, his secretaries, and some of the volunteers from the religious community met in the communal dinning room. Before pastries and coffee were served, the archbishop addressed the volunteers: "I congratulate you, Brother Ignacio, and all the sisters and other volunteers, with the splendid job you're doing. It's important that the church start paying more attention to the unfortunate people of Soacha. It behooves us to bring them into our fold before the Protestant evangelical churches proselytizes them. Colombia is, and must remain, a Catholic country." Then he blessed the building.

Ignacio was disappointed with the archbishop's words. He had never thought of competing with the American evangelicals, who had grown immensely popular in the country. He had attended services of some of the Protestant churches because he wanted to see for himself what they offered that made so many poor Colombians turn their backs on the Catholic church.

Ignacio disliked how the evangelicals emphasized the devil, sin, and punishment of those who deviated from a righteous path. He thought they wielded guilt as a weapon to control their flocks. Furthermore, they reminded him of the old guard of the Catholic church, which instilled fear in their converts as a way to make them more devout. The longer Ignacio remained in the church, the more convinced he became that Jesus Christ was being used as an instrument of oppression.

He despised the obtuse message of the pompous archbishop, but he managed to restrain his tongue and be diplomatic. "Your Grace," he said to the dignitary before he left, "your visit means so much to all of us. Your endorsement of our social programs will allow us to keep working for the people of Soacha."

Around that time, there was a knock one day on the parish house door. On the other side of the door stood a boy who appeared to be around ten years old. "I'm hungry, Father," he said. Ignacio was not a tall man, but the boy barely came up to his belly button. He was shoeless and so dirty that he was of an indeterminate muddy color. His black hair—straight and lustrous like that of the Indians of the Putumayo—fell stiffly to his shoulders. He was covered in soiled rags, and his smell nauseated Ignacio. He had the gaze of a cornered wild animal.

"Please come in. I'm Father Ignacio."

The boy stood still, as if paralyzed by fear.

"Come to the kitchen," Ignacio said.

The urchin was shaking but he stepped through the doorframe and followed Ignacio into the house. His hands were caked with a brown crust, and the tips of his fingernails were black with dirt. Ignacio didn't ask him to wash his hands. He pointed at the table.

"Sit down," he said.

He unwrapped a tamale he had brought home from

Doña Ana's bakery. The boy looked so famished that Ignacio didn't bother to heat the tamale in the microwave. Ignacio placed it on a dish with a fork. The boy grabbed the tamale with both hands and began taking huge bites. Ignacio worried that he might choke if he kept eating like that. After he finished, the boy looked at Ignacio with that gaze of gratitude he had seen on street dogs when you tossed them a scrap of food. The boy still looked hungry, so Ignacio poured him a glass of milk, which he gulped down, making scary gurgling sounds.

Ignacio sat across the table from the boy while he ate. The boy glanced around the kitchen, as if he were trying to figure out what the different appliances were for. Then his eyes settled on a bunch of bananas on the counter.

"Would you like one?" Ignacio asked. The boy shook his head; underneath the layer of dirt that covered his face, Ignacio thought he saw him blush. Ignacio didn't ask him any questions for fear of frightening him. Slowly, the boy got up from his chair and said, "My name is Guillo." Then he took several small steps toward the stove and inserted himself between it and the wall. He rested his head on his open palm and immediately fell asleep.

Throughout the day, Ignacio checked in on Guillo now and then to make sure he was still there. His sleep was fitful and he convulsed on the bare floor muttering incomprehensible words. At one point Ignacio heard him say, "The snake. The snake. Kill it! Kill the snake."

When Ignacio was ready to go to bed that night, the boy was still lying on the floor, though he seemed to be sleeping more soundly. Ignacio covered Guillo with a couple of wool blankets from his bedroom and turned off the light in the kitchen. The boy's presence comforted him, as if he was giving shelter to a feral puppy dog. Ignacio fell asleep without his usual tossing and turning.

When he woke the next morning, he immediately rushed into the kitchen to check on the boy. He found Guillo sitting at the kitchen table. He had eaten all of the bananas, but it was obvious he was still hungry and was waiting for Ignacio to keep feeding him.

Guillo became a permanent resident of the parish house. At first he didn't mingle with the other people there, but he studied them with curiosity. If anybody tried to talk to him, he'd scuttle away. After a couple of weeks, Guillo finally accepted a change of clothes and shoes. He wobbled in the shoes, as if he had gone shoeless all his life. But not even the most persuasive sisters could make him take a shower.

A month later, Guillo still ate his food very fast, as if afraid somebody was going to take the plate away from him. While he chewed, he looked from side to side as if he thought he was in danger of being caged. Once he swallowed a piece of potato so quickly he began to choke. Fortunately, the cook was in the kitchen and screamed for help. Afterward, Guillo was so embarrassed that days went by before he returned to the kitchen to eat. Ignacio left food on the kitchen table at night, and in the morning there would be no traces of it, except for a dirty dish and an unwashed glass.

Ignacio began to think that Guillo was perhaps one of the children they would never be able to reach. He couldn't believe his eyes one morning when he saw the boy go into the room where reading was taught. Ignacio

left him alone. When Ignacio asked Sister Clotilde how
Guillo was doing in class, she told him, "Father, he's very
attentive. But he's having trouble learning the letters of
the alphabet. I've decided to let him progress at his own
pace. It's obvious he wants to learn."

The persistence of Sister Clotilde paid off. One day,
without being prompted, Guillo sat at the kitchen table
to eat with his face and hands washed. The next time the
nuns were giving haircuts, Guillo got in line and waited
his turn. He got the crew cut the nuns gave to children
with lice.

Then, on his own, Guillo began to sweep the floors,
mop the dining room after lunch, and take the garbage
out at the end of the day. He seemed happy when he was
doing these chores. Ignacio also noticed that the boy liked
spending time in the kitchen watching the nuns prepare
meals. One afternoon a sister asked him, "Would you like
to help peel the potatoes, Guillo?" When he nodded, she
handed him a potato and a peeler; from then on, Guillo
peeled the potatoes that the nuns cooked every day. He
started wearing an apron when he was working in the
kitchen, and the nuns began to refer to him as "our as-
sistant." A proud smile came over Guillo's face when he
heard that title.

One of the sisters gave him a bar of soap, a towel, a
shirt, and another pair of jeans. Guillo started shower-
ing regularly. One morning when Ignacio came into the
kitchen to talk to one of the nuns, he barely recognized
the smiling creature the boy had become. Despite all this
progress, Guillo still only talked when he was spoken to.

Ignacio concluded that despite his scrawny body and
short stature, Guillo must be older than he originally

thought—maybe as old as fourteen. He was also super-naturally strong: he lifted the sacks of potatoes and beans as easily as if they were shopping bags. When word of his strength spread in Soacha, housewives paid him to carry heavy baskets from the market to their homes. He was sought after to move large pieces of furniture, or to lay out bricks to build additions to homes. Guillo tried to give Ignacio the money he earned. The first time this happened Ignacio said, "That money is yours. Use it to buy things you need."

For a while no one knew where he slept, but one of the nuns eventually discovered that he spent his nights on top of the sacks of potatoes in the pantry behind the kitchen. Ignacio instructed the workers in the kitchen not to mention to Guillo that they knew where he slept.

One morning when Guillo was chopping vegetables, Ignacio approached the boy. "Put down the knife and come with me," Ignacio told him softly.

He took the boy to a small room in the back of the house that was furnished with a bed that was sometimes used for guests. Guillo looked at Ignacio with puzzlement.

Ignacio hurried to reassure him: "This is your room, if you want it. You can sleep here and keep your things here too. This is your home."

Guillo smiled shyly and lowered his head. Ignacio had never seen his dark brown eyes sparkle with joy. Without looking up the boy said, "Father, I have to finish peeling the potatoes or Sister Sofía will get angry with me." Then he left the room in a rush.

It was the first time that Guillo had spoken a full sentence to Ignacio.

* * *

Around that time, Ignacio began to hear from some of the women who came to confession how their sons, and sometimes their husbands, but always the males in their family, had suddenly vanished. At first, Ignacio thought these were young men who had run away from home—which was common in Soacha—to avoid their responsibilities of taking care of a family. But then, he read a story in a Bogotá newspaper about a guerrilla who had been killed in Norte de Santander in a battle with the army. The article caught Ignacio's eye because the dead guerrilla was identified as Joaquín Padilla, a resident of Soacha.

The following day, Señora Rita, a parishioner who came to confession every week, said, "I have no new sins to confess since the last time I was here, Father." In a tremulous voice and hesitantly, she added, "I wonder if you saw the story about my nephew Joaquín. My sister Juana died when Joaquín was a baby, so I raised him as my son—my only son." Through the partition, he heard her start to sob softly.

It was not unusual for his parishioners to mix the confession of their sins with the hardships that befell them. He often got the impression that what they wanted was not the absolution of their sins, but to be heard, to be consoled.

"May Joaquín's soul rest in peace," he said. "I never met him, but your news saddens me. I feel your loss. May God give you the comfort you need at this time." Ignacio fell silent, searching for words beyond the clichés he had mouthed; he felt defeated because he knew he could not ease her pain. It distressed him how—when it came to comforting his flock—his words frequently sounded hollow to him, as if he were merely reciting something he had memorized.

Señora Rita's voice brought him out of his reflection. "I admit that Joaquín was a troubled young man, Father. Since he was little I always stressed how important it was for him to get an education, if he wanted to have a better life than mine. But he didn't like school; and he didn't like the jobs he could get. His head was filled with cobwebs and dreams of easy money. Like so many of the young people around here, he joined a gang of drug dealers to finance his vice and impress the girls. But Father," she said with sudden vehemence, "Joaquín was not a guerrilla; he was not interested in politics. If you asked, he couldn't tell you the name of Colombia's president. The thing is," she whispered so low that Ignacio had to press his ear against the panel of the confessional, "two other boys in Joaquín's gang were killed in the same way. We haven't heard much about it because they are orphans, so nobody cares whether they live or die." She paused, as if debating whether to stop or continue unburdening herself. Through the black screen of the confessional she looked troubled and afraid. "They're killing our boys, Father," she blurted out.

"Who's killing them?" Ignacio asked, startled by this revelation. "Why haven't I seen anything in the press about this?"

"Maybe people are afraid to talk about it because they think the military's involved." Ignacio saw her cover her mouth with her trembling hands. He wished he could reach through the screen to touch her. Abruptly, she raised her voice: "I'm an old woman, Father. I want to live the rest of my life in peace. May I have your blessing?"

Ignacio blessed her and asked her to pray for peace of mind and heart. After she left, there were no other people waiting to confess, but Ignacio remained inside the dark booth. His legs refused to move, as if they had become columns of lead. If what he had heard was true—and he didn't have any reason to doubt the veracity of Señora Rita's words, especially in the confessional—he realized they were dealing with something extremely troubling.

Before Ignacio called Lucas that night, he debated whether he should mention what he had learned from Señora Rita. They chitchatted for a while, until Ignacio could no longer contain himself and told Lucas what he had learned. When he finished, he asked, "Have you heard any stories like that happening in Barrio Kennedy?"

"No, I haven't, thank God," said Lucas with alarm. "Please be careful, Ignacio. You could be getting into something very ugly."

Ignacio snapped: "So what do you suggest I do—just forget about it?"

"No, of course not," Lucas said hurriedly, in an apologetic tone. "Just promise me you'll be careful."

Ignacio knew that unless he reassured Lucas, his friend would pester him about it nonstop. "I promise," he said, trying not to sound exasperated. Before they said goodbye, they made plans to see each other that Friday night.

The following morning, Ignacio went to Doña Ana's for his café con leche and buttered roll. Nothing happened in Soacha that she didn't hear about. Her store served as news central for the neighborhood. When she brought his breakfast to the table, Ignacio looked around to make sure no one was within earshot. Bluntly, he asked, "Doña

Ana, do you know anything about the young man from Soacha who was found dead in Norte de Santander?"

She moved her eyes from side to side to indicate she was uncomfortable talking while there were customers around. "Father, I'll stop by the parish house this afternoon to bring you some freshly baked cookies—your favorites. And now," she pointed at a plate of scrambled eggs she had set on the table, "I made these especially for you. I want you to eat. You're working too hard and you need to put on some weight. We cannot afford to have you get sick."

Around five p.m., Ignacio's secretary Maritza knocked on his office door and announced that Doña Ana had arrived with cookies for him. "They're still warm, Father," she said, opening her eyes wide and smiling. "Shall I send her in?"

Doña Ana entered his office and closed the door. She placed a paper bag on his desk. Ignacio invited her to sit down. Without any preamble, she began: "Father, I've heard that a few young men from the barrio have been taken by the military, falsely accused of being guerrillas, and killed by the army."

Ignacio exploded: "Nothing surprises me about this country of ours!" Then, realizing his anger had shaken the baker, he removed his glasses and rubbed his eyes. Lowering his voice to a whisper, he said, "But what's the incentive for the military in this case, Doña Ana? What would they get out of killing these boys?"

She shrugged. "I don't know why the government does anything, Father. But people say a new law was passed that's not common knowledge yet. The soldiers who kill guerrillas in action get four million pesos for each dead subversive. We all know that a life is not worth much in Colombia. There are some greedy people in the army who are taking these boys nobody cares about with false promises, and then killing them, dressing them up as guerrillas, and taking their pictures—which they send to the newspapers and the TV stations." Doña Ana crossed herself. "But there's no proof of anything, Father."

Ignacio felt himself filling up with rage again. He clenched his fists and took a deep breath.

Doña Ana stared at her hands as she fidgeted on the chair. Her next move surprised him: she opened the paper bag, removed a cookie, and took a bite. She pushed the bag gently in his direction.

But Ignacio was too upset to eat. "I'll have a couple for dessert tonight," he said. "You know I dream of your cookies."

She didn't smile, but continued speaking. "My friend Amparo's husband was killed. His name was Alejandro Grisales. He was identified in the news as a guerrilla who was killed in combat. That was over a year ago, Father. Since then, these killings have become more common. Somehow I thought you'd heard about it."

He shook his head. "How come no one has mentioned this to me? Don't people trust me?"

"You know how it is, Father: when people think the military is involved, they whisper about it." She paused. "I knew Alejandro since he was a boy in my hometown in Huila. He was a responsible family man. He worked hard in construction to make sure his family ate every day." With sarcasm that was unusual for her, she added, "He was as much a guerrilla as I am, Father Ignacio."

She reached across the desk and grabbed his hand, trying to control her tears. "It's very scary, Father," she said. Then she quickly pulled her hand back and stood up. "I have to return to the bakery. I can't leave Lucila alone for too long. She's still learning the ropes."

"Thank you for the cookies," he said. "God bless you for your kindness."

As soon as he was alone in the room, he knew he had to pay a visit to Amparo, though he knew he would not be able to console her. In his experience, only people who were near death could be consoled—if they had faith and believed they were soon going to be with God. Numerous times, Ignacio had witnessed how grief turned life into a hell of flames that burned and burned until it killed the bereaved.

Around seven a.m., Ignacio stopped by the bakery for directions to Amparo's house. She lived up a steep hill above Soacha; the road to her house was unpaved. Fortunately, it hadn't rained in a few days.

There were children playing outside and street dogs scavenging for food in the piles of garbage. Young men on roaring motorcycles sped up and down the hill. Ignacio had wandered into lawless territory, but he was wearing his frock, so he wasn't overly concerned about his safety: the cassock was still respected in these parts.

It was a cloudless sunny afternoon; a gentle breeze blew in cold air from the peak of the tallest mountains in the distance. Despite the fact that Ignacio had been feeling poorly lately, and losing weight though he wasn't dieting, the brisk walk up the hill had invigorated him.

He walked around for almost half an hour. Finally,

he recognized Amparo's house. Doña Ana had instructed him to look for a solitary house that abutted a large rock on a street corner. The walls were made of wood, and the roof of tin slabs was painted cobalt blue. The color of the roof was the only cheerful thing about the place.

The front door was open, letting sunlight into the house. Ignacio knocked on the door and peeked in. "Good afternoon," he called. The floor was made of cement, but all the partition walls were made of disparate pieces of wood. One of the interior walls was bamboo.

From the back of the house a woman entered the room. She seemed familiar, as if he had seen her in the background of the crowd who attended Sunday Mass. Two girls followed her.

"Father Ignacio!" the woman exclaimed when she recognized him. She looked embarrassed that he had caught her unprepared. She said to the girls, "You know Father Ignacio. You've seen him say Mass on Sundays."

He smiled at the girls, who still didn't seem reassured by their mother's words. Amparo waved him in. "Please, Father, come in." She began smoothing down her hair, and brushed off the front of her blouse and skirt.

"Please excuse me for barging in like this," he said.

"Our humble house," she replied, lowering her gaze, "is your house, Father. Our doors are always open to you; you don't have to tell us in advance. Especially not you, *padrecito*, who does so much for the people."

Amparo pointed to a rocking chair—the best chair in the living room—and he took it. She sat on a wooden chair. The two girls crouched on the floor at their mother's feet, one on each side of her. They wore their black hair in ponytails and had on matching pink blouses with yellow flowers, faded jeans, and sneakers. Amparo was wearing mourning clothes. She seemed nervous and puzzled by his visit, as if she wasn't used to receiving visitors.

Breaking the awkward silence, she said, "May I offer you a cup of coffee?"

"Please don't go through the trouble," he said.

"It's no trouble at all, Father." She got up and hurried out of the room.

In the silence that fell upon the room, Ignacio became aware of *vallenato* music playing in the back of the house. The girls continued to peer at him. While he was wondering how to engage them in conversation, he noticed a flat-screen TV on the wall. Over the TV set there was—as if to shelter it from the rain—a curious roof in the shape of an inverted V. Three green plastic chairs were placed on each side of the television set. It was almost as if the family had built a shrine for the appliance. To the right of the TV was a framed photo of a handsome young man wearing a military cap. *That's Alejandro*, he thought. The photo, cropped slightly below his Adam's apple, showed he was wearing a soldier's shirt and jacket. His head was turned three-quarters to the side, so only one eye was visible—its intense gaze seemed to question Ignacio's presence.

He shifted his attention to the wall on the left. It was decorated with two large posters of Niagara Falls; the bright colors relieved the drabness of the room.

Amparo returned and handed him a cup of black coffee. Before he took a sip, he said, "I came to offer you my condolences for Alejandro's death."

The woman's eyes became brilliant and wet, but she made no sound. Ignacio didn't mention the army or what he had heard about other deaths. Though mother and

daughters remained quiet, Ignacio sensed that the three
women knew why he was there.

The humility expressed in their silence moved him.
"I want you to know that I feel your pain." As usual the
words sounded hollow and arrogant to him. How could
he know their pain? What he felt was anguish at his im-
potence and rage toward the assassins. Ignacio closed his
eyes and bowed his head. He became still and remained
silent; the vallenato music, which continued nonstop,
was now almost a balm.

Ignacio was fully absorbed in his own thoughts when
he heard Amparo begin: "Alejandro and I lived together,
Father. But he talked all the time about marrying me. If
they hadn't killed him, he would have done it." Ignacio
opened his eyes and found her staring at him, without
blinking. "I met him when I was eighteen years old. Alejandro was four years older than me. He was still in the
army, but he was just six months short of finishing the
mandatory service."

Ignacio had never grieved deeply over anyone. His
parents had died of a virulent strain of the flu while he
was at Javeriana University. He felt guilty that he had
not returned to the farm, even for a short visit to see his
sisters, who were now married and had built homes for
their families on the land. Indeed, after his parents died
he had experienced more guilt than grief. At what point,
he wondered, had his heart turned as hard as stone? He
knew he had tried to treat his parishioners with compassion; sometimes they told him they were comforted by
his concern for them. *But am I capable of truly loving
another human being deeply?* He knew he had loved only
one person: Lucas. Ignacio tried to imagine what it would

be like to lose Lucas suddenly, tragically, unjustly. Perhaps only then might he know something resembling the crushing desolation he sensed dwelled in this woman's heart. He wanted to say something to her, but what? *I've loved a man too.*

Amparo rescued him: "I like tall men, so when I met Alejandro I fell for him." She let out a giggle, which seemed to surprise her. "When he was discharged from the army, Alejandro and I left for the jungle in Caquetá. It was during the time that if you cleared a plot of land, and planted legal crops, the government gave you a title of property. We were in the jungle for five years. Our first daughter, Angelina, was born there." She gestured at the girl, who blushed and looked away. "But it was a hard life, Father. So we decided to sell the land and move to Bogotá. With the money we got, we bought this house." She waved her hands around the room where they sat. "Then Yokaira was born. Alejandro didn't want his children to go hungry. He wanted the girls to go to school and have a better life than we had had because we had little education. I only finished the fifth grade; I had to go to work as a domestic to help my parents. Before he went into the army Alejandro had learned to drive. He found a job driving a truck that transported materials for construction. He had to work long days, and often weekends, but I was happier here than in the jungle—which is a good place for children, if you want them to grow up like monkeys."

The girls laughed and Ignacio could not repress a chuckle.

"Girls, show some respect to Father Ignacio," Amparo said. Then she continued: "Alejandro loved soccer, as do

I. On Sundays we'd go to see Millonarios, which was our favorite team." She smiled ruefully. "I'm sorry I'm boring you with all these details."

Ignacio shook his head. The girls giggled when they realized his discomfort. He felt ashamed to be intruding on Amparo's suffering. It was obvious that, though Alejandro had been dead for over a year, they still grieved for him intensely.

Amparo went on: "Alejandro lost his job as a driver because he was in an accident. Our savings didn't last long. If we didn't own this house we would've ended up on the street. Alejandro looked and looked for a job but nothing came up. He came home so excited the day somebody he knew from the army offered him a job on a farm near Neiva. It was almost a day away by car, so he would come to see us every other week. I didn't want him to go away and leave us alone, but when you're poor you just have to take whatever you can get. I packed an army bag with some clothes and things he'd need for his personal hygiene. The day he left, Alejandro said he would be back soon, kissed the girls, and went down the street to meet the man who was going to drive him to the farm. As he walked away, I yelled, 'Please call me when you get there tonight!' He had just turned twenty-eight years old, Father." Her voice broke and she let out a piercing sob. Her daughters rushed to her side, embraced her, and began to cry. "Now, now, girls," she said, gently pushing them away. "Compose yourselves. What's Father Ignacio going to think of us?"

The girls returned to their places on the floor. Amparo burst out, "Father Ignacio, they killed my Alejandro over a year ago! When he didn't call that night, I tried his cell phone but it was turned off. I wasn't too worried yet. I tried again the next day and still no answer. Two days went by, and then, on the third morning, I was watching the TV news at noon, the girls were in school—thank God—when they showed a photo of Alejandro, dead, dressed in military fatigues. Then they showed other dead men. At first I thought it had to be a mistake. I began to scream when the TV announcer said these men were guerrillas killed in military action against the government."

Ignacio clenched his fists in rage, but remained silent.

"Two days later, Alejandro's friend told me that the corpses of half a dozen guerrillas killed in battle had arrived in the morgue. And that he had identified Alejandro among them. They had shot him eight times. The top of his head was like an exploded pomegranate." Amparo paused. "The photos of the dead men began to appear in the newspapers the next day. And there was Alejandro, dead, on the ground, with his eyes open but without expression, like the eyes of an old doll. The photo showed him holding a rifle in his right hand." Suddenly she screamed: "The bastards didn't even know he was left-handed!" Amparo fell silent.

The vallenato music that had been playing on the radio all along was now replaced by a pop song.

Angelina cried out, "That's father's favorite song by Miguel Mateos!" The two girls jumped to their feet and started dancing and singing, "*Soy un chico de la calle . . .*"

When the song was over the girls sat down again and looked serious.

Amparo said, "Father, there are other cases—not just here in Soacha, but people say in many places in Colombia, especially in Caquetá and the Putumayo. People are

afraid to talk about what's happening for fear they'll be
next. Some of the mothers of the young men who've
been killed have begun to organize in Soacha and Ciudad Bolívar. I don't go to their meetings because I work
as a maid and don't get home until late. Besides, if anything happens to me, who's going to take care of my
girls?"

On the walk back to the parish, Ignacio felt numb. How
could he have been so deaf to something so monstrous
happening under his nose? From the hill, Soacha below
looked different—like a place where a rapacious virus
was destroying all living things. Dusk had set in. The
lights that had begun to illuminate the city did not reassure him. He knew that even dressed as a priest, it was
dangerous to walk alone in this neighborhood after dark.
Ignacio shivered violently when a gust of icy wind swept
past him, from the top of the mountains to the savannah
below.

He started walking faster the closer he got to the parish house. When he closed the front door behind him, he
took a deep breath, which he released in one long single
exhalation. The lights in Maritza's office were off. The
cook had left a covered plate of food for him on top of
the stove. The thought of food made him feel queasy.
Maybe the parish house was not the place for him to be
alone tonight. As he paced the kitchen, he thought about
the late Father Camilo Torres, who had been killed by the
government when he joined the guerrillas. *I should have
joined the guerrillas,* he thought. Except that he was not
an idealist anymore: Ignacio knew that the FARC and
other guerrilla groups were as corrupt and wicked as the

cartels and the paramilitaries protected by the government. There were no good guys in this war.

Ignacio opened a bottle of wine, went to his bedroom, and put on a CD by Julio Jaramillo. The sad romantic songs by his favorite singer usually had a soothing effect on him. Instead, the sounds of the guitar chords accompanying Jaramillo's singing felt like knives ripping his insides. His inner turmoil grew. After he opened a second bottle of wine, he called Lucas. He tried to explain what he had learned during his visit to Amparo's house.

After Ignacio had finished his diatribe against the government, FARC, and the drug-traffickers, Lucas said, "You're slurring your words, Ignacio. I can't understand what you're saying. Tomorrow we'll get together and talk about all this. Don't drink more; go to sleep. Please. Promise me you're going to do that. Under no circumstances should you go out to a bar tonight."

"Right," Ignacio said, unable to hide his irritation. "I'll finish the bottle and go to sleep."

Lucas remained silent, as if he didn't believe him.

Then Ignacio said something he hadn't said to Lucas in a long time: "I love you."

"I love you too," Lucas said. "Good night."

Later that week, Ignacio decided to do something he had been curious about for a while. From Father Alberto, a young priest he had become acquainted with, and who sometimes came over to the parish house for dinner and to gossip about the church, Ignacio had heard about gay bars in Chapinero.

"I confess I've been fascinated with those places for a

long time, but I've avoided going there for fear of being exposed," Ignacio had told Father Alberto.

"I'm surprised that you would be so uninformed about these things. The gay bars in Bogotá crawl with priests in civilian clothes. If you want to go some night, just let me know and I can take you to Pollitos, my favorite bar. The boys in Pollitos are"—he licked one of his fingers—"de-li-cious."

Ignacio had blushed; he'd felt, as he often did with people from Bogotá, like a rube.

"Anyway," Father Alberto had continued, "these bars are a safer way to meet *chicos* than to look for sex in flea-ridden dives, where many encounters end up in robbery, beatings, and sometimes, as I'm sure you've read about, in fatal stabbings. If you like, I could introduce you to some boys I know. They can be a handful, but I'm sure you can handle them."

Ignacio had learned to drive and had bought a car with donations from outside the parish. Some members of the clergy thought that Ignacio's car was too ostentatious for a priest from a barrio, but Ignacio didn't care.

He drove to Chapinero, glad to find that the traffic was light. It had finished drizzling and the streetlights were reflected in the droplets on the windshield and the glass windows of the buildings he passed. A full moon had come out, golden and naked in the sky, highlighting the dew on the wet grass along the islands in the middle of the avenue. The trees were heavy with mist as he got closer to Pollitos. Ignacio was nervous but excited. The way Father Alberto had explained it, there was no danger in checking out this place. He told himself that if he hit it off with one of the young men, he was willing to act on the attraction. If he was honest with himself, sex with Lucas nowadays—though Lucas was always enthusiastic and inventive, constantly surprising him with new tricks—seldom aroused him. *I will be careful not to catch the virus,* he told himself. *I won't have unprotected sex.*

As soon as he stepped into the bar, Ignacio fell under the spell of the relentless beat of the music, the clinking of ice in glasses, the smell of marijuana, the men kissing and fondling each other passionately in the open. The promise of something thrilling was intoxicating; the electric gleam in the eyes of many of the patrons suggested they were high on drugs. The energy of the place was so heady that Ignacio had to tell himself he would stop drinking as soon as he noticed he was slurring his words; he was adamant about not driving back home drunk.

The paranoia of running into someone who would recognize him vanished. He stood at the bar, sipping his whiskey and soda and watching the dance floor. It made him sad when he realized he had danced so few times in his life, and never with a man. When he was a boy, Ignacio and his sisters would dance during religious festivals. Was there really no other time in his life? Ignacio shook his head to cast aside the melancholy that suddenly overcame him. He turned to the left, to focus on something else, when he noticed a door at the back of the dance floor through which men alone, or in couples, passed, disappearing into the darkness. When they finally emerged they looked a little disheveled and sometimes sweaty, but relaxed, happy. Ignacio wanted to explore the dark room, and he had been so engrossed in the scene that he hadn't noticed a young man who had moved in his direction and now stood in front of him, blocking his view. His impudence startled Ignacio. He was about to ask this stranger not to block his view, but then changed his mind when he saw how beautiful the man was. Though he was smiling, there was an air of danger about him. Ignacio was surprised that he found it so appealing.

"How about buying me a drink, *papi*?" the man said brazenly. "My name's Rafael. I want to drink whatever you're drinking."

Rafael was of average height, muscular, wore torn jeans and a tight long-sleeved T-shirt that emphasized his muscles. He wore his hair in a ponytail and was handsome in a rugged way. His black eyes, set close together, peered at Ignacio with such intensity that he knew he would have trouble saying no to this young man—now, or ever. Ignacio ordered him a whiskey.

They chatted for a while, Ignacio feeling awkward. He was in the middle of explaining that it was his first time at Pollitos, when Rafael leaned in his direction, grabbed Ignacio by the crotch, and purred, "How about going to a motel and fucking our brains out?"

That first night, when they were naked in the motel room next door to Pollitos, and Ignacio saw Rafael's huge erect penis, and Rafael with one deft gesture removed the elastic band that held his hair, a mass of obsidian hair cascading down and brushing over Ignacio's face, Ignacio knew he was lost. Rafael dropped on the bed, planted his feet on the ground, extended his hand to Ignacio, and whispered, "Come here, *papi*. I'm going to give you the best blow job you've ever had."

Not long after that first encounter, they began seeing each other sometimes two or three nights in a row. Rafael had awakened in Ignacio a complete surrendering of his body and—this frightened him—of his mind. He cared about nothing but being with Rafael, touching him, dragging his tongue, as if it were a sponge, over Rafael's body, drinking his moisture, squeezing him in his arms until his chest hurt, kissing him in orifices where his tongue had never been before, listening raptly to the things Rafael said, and the way he said them.

For the first few times they met, Rafael demanded payment before they went to bed. He would count the bills at least twice before sticking them inside his shoes. Later, when Rafael did not ask to be paid first, Ignacio would hand him a generous sum before he left the motel room. On the nights when he was particularly satisfied, Ignacio would leave larger sums than perhaps he could afford. Because of his ignorance about the rules in Rafael's world, he started to think that it was possible he was more than a john to Rafael; that perhaps they were having a romantic relationship, and that this young man cared about him. Ignacio believed that there might be a true love connection between them: a tenderness, an affection, a fiery lust that seemed to be reciprocal. Rafael made Ignacio feel desired, younger, even optimistic.

Ignacio kept his growing involvement with Rafael from Lucas. He knew Lucas would be hurt if he found out about it. *Sooner or later*, he thought, *without telling him about it, he'll see that I've fallen in love with another man.* Then, and only then, Ignacio decided, would he tell Lucas the truth.

One Monday at ten a.m., as Ignacio parked in front of Archbishop Mota's residence, he wondered whether he should have let Lucas convince him that the worst thing he could do was tell the archbishop what he had learned about the men who had disappeared in Soacha. Ignacio had shaken His Grace's hand a couple of times, but had never had a private moment with him. The archbishop was not known as a progressive, or someone particularly interested in social justice.

To prepare for his visit, Ignacio had met with two members of the Mothers of Soacha. Doña Raquel, who acted as the leader, had told him, "They're taking the boys who will go anywhere with the promise of easy money for doing odd jobs. You know the type, Father: hip-hop thugs, drug addicts. They are the ones the narcos seduce with the lure of working as bodyguards and protecting their operations. As a bonus, the narcos promise them all the drugs and liquor they want, and lots of girls— for free. The military offers them an even more attractive deal: legal jobs in addition to the promise of wiping out their criminal records."

Ignacio was led through a series of well-kept rooms to a small gym with elliptical machines where he found Archishop Mota working out with a muscular young personal trainer wearing sweatpants and a tight-fitting T-shirt.

"Please come in, Father Ignacio," he called. "John and I have just finished our workout."

The trainer handed the archbishop a towel, which he used to wipe the sweat off his face and then dry his hands. He pointed to an area with a couple of comfortable-looking chairs, shook Ignacio's hand, and sat down. The trainer handed him a paper cup filled with water. He drank the contents in one gulp and then said, "John, this is Father Ignacio, the pastor of Soacha, one of the bright new stars of the church."

The trainer smiled. "Pleased to meet you, Father."

"That's all for today, John," Archbishop Mota said. "I'll see you tomorrow at the same time."

They were left alone, and Ignacio heard classical music playing softly through the speakers in the ceiling. The large room had no windows, though it was illuminated with track lights. The door opened again and a uniformed maid came in and quickly set a cup of black coffee on a small table next to Ignacio's chair. He thanked her, picked up the cup, and sipped the sweet black coffee. It was very fresh and aromatic. The woman left the room without once looking up.

Archbishop Mota said, "I have a personal trainer because I think that's the best way to work out. If you just exercise not knowing what you're doing, it's not good. My goal is to lose a little bit of weight." He patted his stomach. "You know, after one turns fifty the termites start moving in."

Ignacio chuckled; Archbishop Mota was known for his sense of humor.

"So, I understand that you want to talk to me about one of your projects in Soacha. I want you to know, Father Ignacio, that your good reputation precedes you. It's come to my attention that in a short time you've gained the respect and love of your parishioners and you've achieved remarkable things. In particular, I admire very much the work you've done with the displaced youth that keep arriving in Bogotá. Those poor unfortunate souls need all the help we can give them. You're a credit to our church, Father."

"Thank you, Your Grace." Ignacio felt like he was blushing but could do nothing to control it.

"So, how can I help you today? Are you thinking about opening another home? A new school? A soup kitchen? All these projects interest the church."

It had been hard to get this chance to talk to Archbishop Mota in person, so Ignacio immediately launched into the stories he had heard about the men who had disappeared lately and then been reported as guerrillas killed in combat. As he talked about his visit to Alejandro's family, and then told some of the other stories he'd heard at the confessional, from Señora Rosa and other parishioners, Ignacio saw the archbishop's lips set in a thin line. By the time Ignacio finished telling him what he knew about the situation, Archbishop Mota was staring at him blankly, as if Ignacio had suddenly become a stranger. He felt a veil of coldness descend between them.

The archbishop's tone became detached, almost frosty. "I have eyes and ears in the community, Father Ignacio, and I've heard some of these stories too. Recently, I've seen the same stories appear on television. But to insinuate that our military and police have anything to do with these disappearances is dangerous. It doesn't behoove a man of the cloth to make these charges with absolutely no proof to back up any of these libelous accusations. Men of the cloth like us have to be careful about the things we say because people tend to pay attention to us when we speak. Until these rumors have been proven to be facts in a court of law, we're just talking about allegations that can be very damaging. You're young, Father Ignacio. And youth is the time to be passionate. I sense, too, that you have the passion of a poet: you feel you need inspiration to deliver the message. But you cannot be a good messenger of Christ if you let your impulses rule you. Above all things, you must be prudent . . . and humble. Hubris is unbecoming in a priest—it gets in the way of our work. You must pray for humility. You will find peace of mind not in thinking but in praying. As servants of the church, we are just vessels through whom the word of God is delivered. Remember always that you're just a deliverer, not the writer of the message." When the archbishop finished, he smiled. Ignacio shivered.

The meeting left Ignacio so distressed that later that night he couldn't eat his dinner. He thought about going to Pollitos to meet Rafael. Instead, he poured himself three fingers of whiskey and sank into his favorite chair in the living room. But his anguish grew; and when Lucas called around ten p.m., he didn't answer his good night call. Then Ignacio did what he often did when he was tormented and felt defeated: he put on the DVD of *The Color Purple*. As always happened, he was soon lost in Celie's story. He was comforted by how, despite the injustices she suffered, Celie managed to survive and go on—which was what he struggled the most with . . . simply going on.

When he woke up in the morning, he was still in his chair in the living room, with the TV on.

CHAPTER SIX
BARRIO KENNEDY
2008

LUCAS HAD NO TROUBLE ADMITTING TO HIMSELF that he lacked Ignacio's spirit of sacrifice. He was aware that for a priest he enjoyed material comforts too much. He liked to watch old movies until the early-morning hours, which caused him to wake up late some days to say Mass. When it came to dealing with the hierarchy of the church, he avoided contradicting his superiors whenever his position in Kennedy might be jeopardized. Sometimes Lucas thought of himself as cowardly.

He accepted that, by comparison to the magnitude and scope of Ignacio's projects in Soacha, his accomplishments in Barrio Kennedy were modest. Lucas had never considered himself an envious person but now found he was troubled by Ignacio's spreading fame in Bogotá. He prayed that his envy would go away, but it didn't. When he mentioned it during confession, his Father confessor said, "Well, Ignacio's ambitions are larger than yours. And they have to be: the people of Soacha have much less than the people of Kennedy. If you pray for your envy to dissipate, and it doesn't, then try to do more for your flock—if you can. Maybe you'll have to accept that envy is a part of your nature that you'd like to change."

* * *

Lucas had tried to be a modern priest—friendly, not stern. He wore black jeans, short-sleeved white shirts, and sneakers, except to deliver Mass. His only concession to tradition was to always wear the collar. He had also modernized some of the rituals in his church. Instead of playing solemn religious music during Mass, he introduced singers with guitars, who performed upbeat Christian songs—like the Protestant evangelical churches did. Inspired by the example of Father Jean Baptiste-Marie Vianney, he wrote his sermons in the vernacular and addressed people's everyday problems. To be a good Christian, he stressed in his homilies, all that was required was to undergo an interior transformation that was reflected outwardly in the ways people treated others and helped the neediest among them.

By the time Lucas had finished his studies at Javeriana University, he had noticed that many Catholics were losing their passion for the church because what they were being taught was so ethereal. Yes, it was true that Jesus was resurrected, and the Virgin Mary gave birth through an immaculate conception—these were fundamental pillars of Christianity he embraced unquestioningly. But he knew that they were also not the main issues regular people grappled with in real life, because they were so abstract that they no longer meant anything to many believers.

Instead of saying to his parishioners, "Love thy brother" (words which made him blush because they sounded hollow to him), he would say things like, "Visit your old relatives who live alone and forgotten—even if you dislike them."

On some level he remained proud of Ignacio's accomplishments. His friend began to appear in the press regularly, and there were segments on TV about his most ambitious social projects. Volunteers started arriving in Soacha from far away, and donations poured in from Colombians and others abroad who had learned about what Ignacio was doing. But for the first time in the years they had known each other, he also felt resentful of Ignacio, whose growing celebrity made Lucas feel small. In uncharitable moments toward himself, he thought he was just like the little mice who always scuttled along the base of the walls, never daring to cross a room down the middle for fear of being squashed. So many donations had come in for Ignacio's projects that Soacha's parish house was rebuilt and new offices were added; he had a full-time staff of five people.

But Lucas's love for Ignacio was much greater than his envy. He could understand as a common human weakness that Ignacio's success had gone a bit to his head. Furthermore, Lucas worried about Ignacio's health: he was doing the work of a dozen men; Lucas feared that if he kept up this frantic pace he would fall ill from the stress. Ignacio had always been intense, but now he was functioning constantly at full speed.

Lucas began to notice that the more involved Ignacio got in new social projects, the more erratic and volatile he became. His raging outbursts alarmed Lucas. At times, Ignacio acted more like a politician than a man of the cloth. Was it possible, he began to wonder, that Ignacio cared more about people's physical needs than their spiritual state? He seemed to have lost all patience with the conservative policies of the church's hierarchy and the corruption of Colombia's so-called democratic institutions. Ignacio often seemed like an active volcano about to erupt. He talked nonstop about how men in Soacha were being disappeared by the military; Lucas was afraid that finally something had snapped in his friend's mind and he was in danger of rubbing important people the wrong way. "Ignacio," he would plead, "I want you to be very careful. If you make certain people your enemies, your life could be in danger."

"What am I supposed to do?" Ignacio would counter. "Not talk about it? If I can't mention it to you—to *you*, for God's sake!—whom am I going to confide in?"

"Of course you can talk to me about what's happening, which sounds horrible, but you're very tense and if you obsess about this situation it's going to affect your health."

"How important is my fucking health? My parishioners are dying all around me and I have to pretend I don't hear or see anything? I'd rather be dead than do that."

Lucas didn't want to upset Ignacio further. As calmly as he could, he said, "Ignacio, you're the most important person in my life. If anything happened to you, it would be very hard for me to go on."

"Fine," Ignacio replied. "I won't talk anymore about the people being disappeared. I know how squeamish you are."

"You can call me a coward if you like. I admit I'm one when it comes to preserving my life. I—"

"*I, I, I* . . . You sound like a broken record," Ignacio interrupted. "I won't fucking mention any of this to you again. Okay? Okay? Are you happy now?"

For years, Lucas had been aware that Ignacio drank more

than he did. Every few weeks or so, Ignacio would go on binges that lasted a couple of days. When Lucas mentioned his concern about how his drinking seemed to have escalated, Ignacio barked, "I have to let off steam somehow." Lucas began to wonder if Ignacio was taking drugs. When he came for dinner on Friday nights, he was often tipsy before they finished their meal. In fact, Ignacio frequently seemed more interested in the wine than the food. When Lucas gave him disapproving looks, Ignacio would snap, "What? Wine is nutritious; it's full of vitamins and good for the blood." But one night he finally conceded, "Lucas, if I don't get smashed every night, I can't sleep. And I need to sleep at least a few hours so I can function the next day."

When he stayed over they slept in the same bed, but eventually they stopped having sex. Lucas missed the old intimacy. When he brought up the subject, Ignacio replied, "If you miss sex with me, why don't you find somebody else to satisfy your needs?"

His words hurt Lucas deeply. Though Lucas had sexual needs like any other healthy priest his age, years before he had decided he would be monogamous, even if Ignacio went to bed with other men. Lucas considered himself old-fashioned. He couldn't have sex with a man unless he loved him, and the only man he had ever loved, and still loved, was Ignacio. He didn't want to lose Ignacio; so if Ignacio wanted to be promiscuous, Lucas accepted that was the price he would have to pay.

Lucas decided to start joining Ignacio when he went to the gay bars in Chapinero. Lucas was less anxious if he was with him, and if Ignacio got too drunk, Lucas could drive him back home. Most Friday nights around eleven, Lucas would drive the two of them from Kennedy to the bar district. They dressed almost exactly the same, the way most gay couples did: jeans, sneakers, and black leather jackets.

The first time they went into a bar together, Lucas was surprised to discover that the bouncers at Pollitos knew Ignacio and treated him with deference. Once they went inside the dark, smoky space, where the music and the people were loud, Lucas discovered that the bartenders and waiters treated Ignacio as a regular. A handful of the most attractive young men who patronized the bar greeted him with, "Good evening, Father Ignacio," or, "Nice to see you, Father." Lucas was shocked that Ignacio had become so public about being gay; he was sure this would bring nothing but trouble.

A few young men brazenly came over and asked Ignacio to buy them a drink. It was obvious to Lucas that this was not the first time this had happened. The way his friend gulped down drink after drink made Lucas uncomfortable. When Ignacio spotted an attractive young man looking in his direction, he'd send him a drink. All the young men accepted the drinks he sent them, and a few came over to thank him and keep him company. Some flirted with Lucas. Though he sometimes found them attractive, Lucas had made up his mind that he would not take anyone home. In the early 2000s, AIDS was rampant in gay circles in Colombia, but most Colombians refused to wear condoms; many still thought AIDS was a "gringo disease."

Every night, when he said his last prayers of the day, Lucas prayed that Ignacio would be careful. He was certain that many of the young men in the bars Ignacio patronized had the virus, even if they still looked healthy and attractive.

And yet, as much as Lucas disliked the scene, it was unthinkable to leave Ignacio alone in that world. More and more often, by the end of the night Ignacio was completely drunk. Lucas would drive him home and stay overnight to make sure Ignacio did not decide to go back out again. It saddened him that Ignacio did not seem to find any joy in these escapades. There was something depressing in these nights out.

Lucas knew Ignacio was being self-destructive in other ways as well. Around that time there was a scandal reported in the media about Father Juan, a young gay priest they had run into at the bars. Father Juan had taken a hustler home to share with his lover and woke up to find himself on his bed in a pool of blood, having been stabbed many times. His lover, lying next to him, had also been stabbed multiple times and was dead. Father Juan had managed to call the police before he passed out again. The burglars had stripped the parish house of valuables and had stolen gold candelabras, silver vases, and crosses from the church.

Lucas and Ignacio talked about this incident, and Lucas wondered if that was the reason Ignacio had begun to have sex exclusively with a hustler named Rafael. Ignacio would go to Pollitos and wait until Rafael had drunk and drugged and danced and socialized with his friends, then Rafael would leave with him. Lucas didn't trust Rafael's driving any more than he trusted Ignacio's. By the time they left in the early hours, both Ignacio and Rafael were completely drunk.

Late one Friday night, on the drive back home, Rafael

brought out a pipe and he and Ignacio smoked something that produced a foul chemical smell.

"What is that?" Lucas asked.

"It's meth," Rafael said. "You should try it, Father. It's the best."

Several days later Lucas drove over to Soacha in the afternoon to have a talk with Ignacio. It was sunny out, so Lucas suggested they sit outside for coffee in the little garden behind the parish house. In a shaded patch, Ignacio had planted some sweet cicely seeds a friend had brought him from Germany. The bushes were crowned with white flowers that produced an inebriating fragrance like that of powdered anise; the piquant aroma cleared Lucas's head.

After they were served coffee, Lucas said, "You look like you've lost weight, Ignacio. Are you okay?" Ignacio had always been on the thin side, but now his face sometimes looked gaunt. Though Lucas knew the answer, he asked, "Are you still smoking crystal meth? You know," he added hesitatingly, "I've done some research and I found there are discreet rehabs where people go to get off drugs."

Ignacio hit the table with his fist, almost knocking over the cups of coffee. "I work very hard. What's wrong with having a little harmless fun? What about all those drunken priests we know? Why is it okay to be a drunk, but not to have a little fun with drugs?"

"Methamphetamine is not harmless," Lucas said. "I've seen what it does to people in Kennedy."

Ignacio leaped from his chair and started pacing the yard. "It's dangerous if you abuse it; I don't abuse it!"

he yelled. "I just do it a little with Rafael, on weekends. Where's the harm in that? You're becoming a holier-than-thou bore." He kicked a rosebush and petals scattered to the ground.

With the palms of his hands, Lucas motioned to Ignacio to lower his voice. He hadn't seen him so upset in a long time. Ignacio returned to his chair. When the sun emerged from behind a patch of clouds, Lucas noticed in the bright light that Ignacio's upper lip was puckered, his cheeks were sunken, and his face had a greenish tint. Lucas didn't want to upset him further, but this was his chance finally to discuss Rafael. "I don't like him," he said flatly. "He's not a good influence on you. Please try to put some distance between the two of you."

Ignacio sat very still. His shoulders drooped, making him look smaller than he was. His eyes were closed; when he opened them slowly, thick tears ran down his cheeks. "I'm in love with Rafael," he whispered, trembling. "I can't help it. Asking me to stop seeing him is like asking me to stop breathing—my heart would die." He took a deep breath, his lips quivered. "So he likes drugs and I have to pay him for sex. How's that different from all those other boys in the bars? Lucas, what else could Rafael have become in a place like Bogotá? I know you've already made up your mind and see no redeeming qualities in him. But where's your Christian compassion? You know," he continued, his voice rising again, "it's easy to have compassion for the old and children and animals. What about the ones who are not pitiful, do not look vulnerable, or are adorably cute? Once, I asked Rafael why he lived the way he did. You want to know what he said?" Ignacio gave Lucas an accusatory look that made

him feel like a bad person for having raised the question. "He told me that his father was a criminal—an
assassin-for-hire, in fact—and that growing up Rafael
thought that was the only option open to him. To Rafael
his father was a glamorous man, somebody to admire; he
always had money and drugs and all the pretty women he
wanted, and people respected him for that."

Ignacio's words made Lucas angry; he felt he was listening to a stranger he didn't like. It upset Lucas to be
eaten by jealousy, a feeling that he had always tried to
keep in check because he thought it was one of his ugliest
character defects. Even so, he was too wounded to feel
sympathy for Rafael. He failed to see anything appealing
about the man—except his good looks. He didn't care
that Ignacio and he didn't have sex with each other anymore, but he had always assumed blindly that he would
be the only man Ignacio would ever love. Lucas knew
that no matter what happened between them, he could
never love another man. He was feeling so confused he
didn't trust himself. He got up from his chair.

"I have to go back to Kennedy," he said. Before he
left the garden, he added, "I hope at least you're having
safe sex with him. I would be surprised if he didn't have
AIDS."

Ignacio got up from his chair too and came very close
to Lucas. "So what if I have fallen in love with an un-
worthy, cruel, angry, unfeeling, selfish boy deadened by
drugs and disrespectful of human life?" Spit flew out of
his mouth as he said these words. "You know what he
told me when I suggested he should continue his education so he could get a good job? He said, 'Ignacio, when
you come from a place where people are worth less than

a dead rat flattened by a truck on the road, where count-
less children and old people die on sidewalks and nobody
even knows their names, it's fucking insane to want to
become a person with regular aspirations. Where I come
from, young men don't want an education, they want
guns, drugs, easy money, and girls with big tits who desire boys who can offer them those things. What do you
want from me, anyway? To be your boyfriend and live
my life in the shadows, pretending to be your best friend,
because we could never love each other out in the open?
Don't talk to me about boyfriends and lovers; I reject
those terms. The only thing I have now is my freedom,
and I don't want to lose it. If love is not about freedom,
then for me it's nothing.'"

"You romanticize him," Lucas replied, realizing he
could not make Ignacio see Rafael for what he was. Or
worse, the possibility that indeed Ignacio saw Rafael for
what he was, but didn't care despite the imminent danger
he was in.

Lucas began to pray for Ignacio every chance he got.
He had not prayed so fervently since the time he had
begged San Martín de Porres to save his arm from being
amputated. But though he had seen over and over how
prayer consoled people, he had never seen it bring about
the miracles people prayed for. In the church, they were
taught that the real miracle of prayer was the consolation
it brought to the sufferers at that moment when they believed blindly in God's compassion, and they surrendered
so completely that they experienced a kind of peace in
letting go and admitting their powerlessness. But that
knowledge no longer appeased him; it was clear that Ig-

nacio was killing himself. Lucas was growing angry with God.

He stopped going to the gay bars on Friday nights with Ignacio. He told himself that maybe his friend needed a good scare before he came to his senses. Lucas had not felt so painfully lonely in a long time. Confession did not bring solace: he could not freely admit to his Father confessor that he had been in love with Ignacio for most of his life, that life without him seemed unthinkable. And the only person who might have consoled him, who might have understood Lucas without judging him—his mother—had been dead for a few years.

Lucas had always marveled at Ignacio's stamina, but it was obvious that Ignacio needed to slow down—he was often hyperexcited and irritated. One day he called Lucas sobbing loudly. This was unusual: Lucas had seen Ignacio cry perhaps three times in the years they had known each other. In between sobs, Ignacio managed to get out, "Rafael has AIDS. He decided to return home to his mother to the town on the coast where he grew up." Ignacio wept uncontrollably. "I love him, Lucas! I don't know if I want to live without him!"

"Remember that there are many people who need you," Lucas said, struggling to remain calm. "They depend on you; you cannot abandon them." But what he wanted to say was, *What about me? Don't you give a damn about how your recklessness affects me too? Could I live without you? Have you thought about that?*

Not long after that conversation, Ignacio began to complain about a general achiness, frequent fevers, and chills. He developed itchy rashes all over his body. Lucas had read about the night sweats and he knew they were often a symptom of HIV. But he couldn't bear to contemplate for more than a few seconds the idea that Ignacio was sick. In the following weeks, Ignacio complained about a persistent cold that never went away. His weight loss was obvious. Lucas tried to console himself that there were new drugs he had read about that prolonged people's lives. He had also heard that the drugs worked for most people, unless the disease was too advanced. He knew that they were expensive in Colombia, but he and Ignacio were no longer poor priests.

Lucas searched desperately for openings to talk to Ignacio about his physical deterioration, but when Ignacio sensed where the conversation was headed, he always cut Lucas off. All their phone conversations ended with Lucas telling Ignacio to make an appointment to see Doctor Ramírez for a checkup. Ignacio always replied, "Don't worry, I will."

Finally, when Ignacio called Lucas to say he had yet another high fever, Lucas said, "You have to go see Doctor Ramírez *today*."

Ignacio replied that he was too weak to get out of bed.

Lucas contacted Doctor Ramírez right away and told him about Ignacio's call.

"If he's too weak to get out of bed, you need to bring him here immediately," the doctor said.

Lucas raced over to Soacha. When he opened the front door, he saw no signs of the people who worked in the parish house. He went directly to Ignacio's bedroom and discovered that the bed was covered in diarrhea and his friend appeared to be unconscious. The bedroom was so fetid that Lucas ran to the window facing the back-yard and opened it wide.

The cold breeze that blew in revived Ignacio. When he recognized Lucas, he said, "I'm sorry to put you through this." He moaned. "I didn't call the cleaning lady because . . . I'm afraid. I didn't want her to see me like this."

"Let's get you cleaned up before we go see Doctor Ramírez," Lucas said. He had always been squeamish about bodily functions, but he managed not to gag while he helped Ignacio undress. Then he undressed himself, lifted Ignacio in his arms, and carried him to the bathroom. Lucas was surprised that Ignacio seemed to weigh no more than the robust toddlers he sometimes baptized. He turned on the hot water and, propping Ignacio against the tiled wall, soaped and rinsed his body.

When they arrived at the doctor's office, Ignacio rushed to the bathroom. Several minutes went by. When the nurse said she was ready to have him fill out some forms, Lucas went to bathroom and knocked on the door. "Go away," Ignacio said.

Lucas snapped, "Let me in, Ignacio, or I'm going to kick the door open!" After he banged on the door loudly a few more times, Ignacio finally opened it: his face was drenched in sweat and there was a look of panic in his eyes.

"I'm okay now," he said. "Let's go home."

"We're not going anywhere until Doctor Ramírez has seen you," Lucas said firmly.

When Ignacio finished filling out the forms, the nurse said, "This will be quick, Father. Now we just need to draw some blood."

Lucas saw the look of panic in Ignacio's eyes, so he

said, "I'll go first." He extended his right arm to the nurse.

A few days later they returned to Dr. Ramírez's office for the results. When they were alone in the office with him, the doctor said, "Father Lucas, you're HIV negative." Lucas did not feel any relief. Although he was almost sure of Ignacio's status, he desperately hoped the doctor would say he was negative too. "But you, Father Ignacio," the doctor said, "you have AIDS. Your immune system is severely compromised."

Ignacio sat quietly.

Doctor Ramírez continued, "As you know, Father Ignacio, HIV is no longer a death sentence. It's treated now as a long-term and manageable illness—something like diabetes. With the new medications, and all the advances in treatment, there's no reason why you shouldn't have a long and productive life."

Ignacio avoided the doctor's eyes. Lucas got the impression his friend didn't understand anything the doctor was saying. With disturbing intensity, his shining eyes stared at Lucas. Dr. Ramírez suggested various treatments, gave Ignacio some prescriptions to fill, and made recommendations about lifestyle changes. "You need to avoid stress, Father, and eat nutritious meals." Then, enunciating each word carefully, he added, "With the medications you'll be taking, you cannot drink alcohol."

Ignacio had nodded and maintained his composure throughout the visit, but when they were in the car in the parking lot, the first thing he said was, "Lucas, promise me you won't tell anybody that I have AIDS. If people find out I'm dying, all funding will stop coming in; all my projects will collapse."

"Of course," Lucas said. "You can count on me." But

he was hurt that Ignacio could even think he might di-vulge his secret.

All at once, Ignacio stopped going out to gay bars, quit smoking methamphetamine and cocaine and drinking al-cohol. The first few days, things got worse and he shook badly for long periods.

"He's detoxing," Doctor Ramírez explained to Lucas when he called to express his concern. "Just make sure he drinks lots of liquids. He needs to be hydrated. In a few days he should be okay."

As the doctor had predicted, Ignacio soon stopped shaking: he became calmer, and did not complain, as if he were resigned to die. Yet he grew paranoid when people stared at him because of his haggard face and thinness.

From the time they had moved to their own parish-es after university, Lucas and Ignacio had usually talked on the phone at least twice a day. Lucas called him first thing every morning to wish him a good day, and one of them—usually Lucas—made sure to call the other at night before they went to sleep. But now they were con-stantly on the phone. Lucas would call to remind Igna-cio to take his medications and to make sure he was not overworking and that he ate nourishing meals. As Igna-cio made changes in his lifestyle, and began to take his medications with regularity, he started to put on weight, and some color returned to his cheeks.

Lucas was beginning to feel hopeful that the disease had been caught before it was too late, and that Ignacio might be spared a humiliating deterioration. Ignacio no longer seemed obsessed with Rafael; at least, he didn't mention him in their conversations.

* * *

One night Ignacio called Lucas in complete hysterics. At first Lucas thought something had happened to Rafael.

"Guillo has disappeared without leaving a trace," Ignacio managed to say through his sobs. "Something awful has happened to him; something tells me Guillo's dead."

As soon as he heard the news Lucas had a bad premonition, but he knew he had to reassure Ignacio. "You don't know that. Let's not jump to conclusions. Maybe he just got on a bus and by mistake ended up far away from Bogotá and is still trying to figure out how to get back."

"Or his guardian angel will pick him up and drop him on his bed safe and sound," Ignacio said scornfully, ending the conversation.

For ten days, Ignacio became frighteningly erratic: he screamed at Lucas on the phone over any perceived criticism, and accused him of coldness and lacking in compassion.

One night Lucas was in his pajamas watching the late news, when Guillo's face appeared on the television screen. Lucas gasped: Guillo was shown on the ground, shot in the face. The announcer identified him as a guerrilla killed in combat against the Colombian army, in the mountains of Norte de Santander.

Since nothing was known about Guillo's relatives, Ignacio, accompanied by Lucas, identified Guillo's corpse in the morgue. Hundreds of people from Soacha attended the funeral Mass. On the phone with Lucas, or in person, Ignacio would launch into scathing tirades against the government and its complicity with the army.

Lucas warned him, "I'm not blind; I agree with you. Some people are aware of what's happening. But be careful when you talk to strangers; you just don't know how far what we say can travel and whose ears it might reach. Nobody who messes with the armed forces in this country is safe."

"I don't care who hears me!" Ignacio yelled. "If they want me to shut up, they'll have to kill me! I can't live the rest of my life like a whimpering mouse, afraid to make a sound. If the army kills me for denouncing them, so be it. At least I'll die with some dignity. That's better than dying because of a stupid virus."

When Ignacio talked like that, he was in a place where Lucas could not reach him. Lucas began to fear that Ignacio might not die of AIDS, but of a bullet to his head. When Lucas was forced to consider the idea of life without his friend, the mere thought was too horrible to contemplate. Lucas felt selfish. In recent years, there had been some days when the never-ending complications of being in charge of a large parish overwhelmed him, and he woke up feeling tired. On those days, being a priest had been the only thing that motivated him to get out of bed. But without Ignacio, Lucas had to admit to himself, attending to the spiritual needs of his flock, the church, even the love of God, would not be enough to keep him going.

Lucas came up with the idea of taking Ignacio for drives on the savannah of Bogotá, and up into the mountains they both loved. Yet even away from the noise of the city, and surrounded by the emerald-green expanses of the Andes, Ignacio remained cocooned in his anger. By the time they drove back to the city late at night under a cobalt sky throbbing with stars, Ignacio would still be immersed in an unrelenting gloom.

One night, as Lucas stopped in front of the rectory in Soacha to drop him off, Ignacio said, "You know when I realized Guillo was truly special? Shortly after he moved into his own room, he came into the house looking happy, with his shirt off. I was in the kitchen having lunch. I was about to tell him he was going to catch a cold if he went around shirtless in the house, when I noticed he had made a bundle of the shirt and inside the bundle there was something fragile. He approached me cautiously, smiling, and uncovered the top of the bundle gingerly to reveal the head of a blackbird. He said, 'I found her on the street, Father. She has a broken wing; she cannot fly. A cat was going to eat her. Can I keep her, Father? Can I?'"

Sensing this was an important story Ignacio wanted to share with him, Lucas rolled down the window on his side and turned off the engine.

"Guillo had never asked me for anything," Ignacio went on. "I figured the bird would live a day or two and that would be the end of it. So I told him he could keep the unfortunate creature. 'I'll make a sling for her wing. She'll fly again, Father,' Guillo said, smiling, happy. Well, I forgot about the bird. One day, as I passed by his room, I heard the distinct song of a blackbird coming from behind the door. I was tempted to open the door to see the bird. But I'd given orders that no one should ever enter Guillo's room without his permission. We knew he kept the room clean because he was constantly taking a broom and a dustpan inside. I decided not to mention to him that I had heard the bird singing. Soon everyone who worked in the house talked about the most beautiful song coming out of Guillo's room. Sometimes, when the bird began to sing, people would interrupt whatever they were doing to listen.

"Late one afternoon I was working in the office when the secretary knocked on the door and said that Guillo wanted to speak to me. I stopped what I was doing and walked to the door to let him in. 'I want to show you something, Father,' he said. I immediately knew it had something to do with the bird and followed Guillo to his room. He opened the door wide enough so he could go in quickly, and then motioned for me to follow him. I was noticing how immaculate his room looked, when I heard Guillo whistle an imitation of a bird's song. I felt a swooping of feathers over my head and then saw the bird perch on the index finger of Guillo's right hand, which he held out in front of him, pointing at me. 'Her name is Mariela,' he said, and then placed the open palm of his left hand on the back of the bird and caressed it. Slowly, he walked toward the door, which I opened for him."

The night had gotten chilly, but Lucas kept the car window down. It had been awhile since Ignacio had been so loquacious. Ignacio took a deep breath and then he spoke faintly, slowly, "I wish you could've seen how careful Guillo was as he descended the steps to the garden. When we were outside, he rubbed his nose against the bird's velvety brown head and then lifted his palm off the bird's back. The blackbird rowed its wings upward and, in a flash, it took to the air."

Ignacio paused, then turned to Lucas and began to talk very deliberately, as if he had mulled over what he was about to say for a long time: "For many years I couldn't find the God of the church through prayer. I want you to know that I finally found a God I can believe in, a merciful God, in the lessons people like Guillo have taught me . . . After that, I stopped fearing God's retribution, as I'd always been taught. The God I found felt compassion for me, for all human beings, because perhaps God—awed by His own creation—for a second had become distracted and made a world that was both heaven and hell at the same time."

Lucas thought Ignacio was done speaking, but he had more to say. "I know that to have faith means to take a leap. But it was a leap I wasn't willing to make. Lucas, I didn't find faith following a logical path of deduction, as I always stubbornly believed I would. If I've found something like faith it was through an accident—Guillo coming into my life."

Ignacio left the car without closing the door or saying good night. Lucas reached over, closed the door, and waited until Ignacio had entered the rectory before he drove off.

AFTER GUILLO WAS KILLED, IGNACIO BEGAN TO drink heavily again. Most of the time when Lucas called him to say good night, his words were slurred, though he tried— with difficulty—to speak clearly. In the background, Lucas could hear the boleros of Julio Jaramillo playing: the guitar strings tugging at the heart, the heartbreak in the voice of the singer, the lyrics that spoke about lost love and despair and a cruel world; to many Colombians these songs were a kind of national anthem. This was the music that Ignacio listened to when he got drunk on aguardiente. Once he kicked back the first shot of the brew, he could not stop. Most nights Ignacio fell into a stupor and lost consciousness until the following day.

When Ignacio's tearful monologues turned into angry rants, Lucas knew he was smoking methamphetamine again. One night he yelled at Lucas: "I've devoted my life to improving the plight of the people in Soacha, yet many here think I'm a transgressor! They would be happy with a priest who was more distant and impersonal, more god-like." His anger worried Lucas. "Why do they criticize me, when all I want is to help them? I drink too much and smoke crystal meth because nothing else can lessen my pain!"

From the beginning of his ministry—and even earlier during his years in school—Ignacio's unrestrained enthusiasms had brushed authorities in the church the wrong way. Lucas understood why there were people in Soacha who disliked Ignacio, just as he knew there were parishioners in Kennedy who disliked him too, because his ideas were more modern than theirs. Yet Lucas was sure the majority of the people in Soacha were grateful to Ignacio. He gave his friend a copy of Mother Teresa's *No Greater Love*, the book he read from every morning as soon as he woke up.

"I wish I had an uncomplicated heart like yours," Ignacio said as he took the book. "It's true she did great things for the poor, but you know the woman was a terror and a tyrant."

"I know she had many flaws," Lucas replied. "That just proves that she was like the rest of us. Perhaps it's even more admirable to do good if you're a sinner."

"Whatever I do for others, I do because I have a conscience," Ignacio snapped. "It has nothing to do with the desire to be good or to be godly. I seldom see goodness around me. Everywhere I look I see more pain than joy, more illness than health, and evil crushing kindness. I've come to the conclusion that your God has a sadistic streak."

At the risk of infuriating him further, Lucas said, "Maybe we end up thinking evil is all there is because it spreads like an infected fistula that rots everything it comes in contact with, whereas goodness has to be earned."

"Whatever!" Ignacio exclaimed. "Your watered-down theology makes me want to puke."

That night Lucas didn't pray to God to save Ignacio from AIDS; he prayed for Ignacio to find some peace. Lucas was afraid that the gloom in Ignacio's soul might be contagious.

The news of Guillo's disappearance was so absurd—how could a boy who hardly understood the world join the guerrillas?—that the media descended upon Soacha, smelling a juicy story. Television crews, radio announcers, and print journalists came to interview Ignacio when they found out Guillo had lived in the parish house.

Lucas pleaded with Ignacio, "Don't talk to reporters; don't get involved in this; don't be reckless."

Ignacio confirmed that Guillo had lived in the parish for two years; but that was all he said to the press. However, to Lucas's horror he began to talk to all who would lend him an ear about the murder of Alejandro Grisales. Once Grisales's killing was mentioned publicly, there was a flurry of stories about other young men throughout Colombia who had been killed by soldiers in similar circumstances.

In the years following his ordination, Lucas had felt racked with guilt for sticking his head in the ground to avoid commenting on the violence in Colombia. He had told himself that feeling empathy for the unfortunate ones and offering social services they lacked in Kennedy was all he could do. But when Ignacio began to denounce the False Positives, as the men who disappeared were now called, he started to wonder if he had always tried to protect the church from controversy because he was satisfied with his pleasant life and did not want to risk changing it.

* * *

The group that called itself the Mothers of Soacha came forward to confirm that the situation had been going on for almost two years, and that their sons and husbands had been killed in circumstances similar to those of Guillo and Alejandro.

Ignacio publicly accused the military of involvement in the matter, and Lucas feared that he was asking to be killed. Ignacio still said Mass every day, but he began to turn over more responsibilities to his volunteers in the parish. Lucas suspected Ignacio had stopped taking his medications, because his physical appearance suggested that the disease was advancing again.

"If you want the situation with the False Positives to stop," Lucas told him, "you need to live. And for that, you need to take your medications."

Ignacio didn't reply, but Lucas could see that the prospect of his own death did not scare him.

They both received a call from Archbishop Mota's secretary requesting a meeting. Lucas thought it was an ominous sign they had been asked to appear before the archbishop together, but he didn't mention this to Ignacio. He had become so volatile that Lucas was frightened of his increasingly explosive outbursts.

They made a plan to go to the meeting together. After coffee was served, and they had chitchatted about the awful traffic, Archishop Mota turned to Lucas and said, "I wanted you to be present at this conversation, Father Lucas, because I know you and Father Ignacio are like Siamese twins. I'm hoping you can help me talk some sense into him."

Lucas squirmed in his chair and clasped his hands. Although he and Ignacio assumed that everyone in the

church in Bogotá knew about the nature of their relationship, it was understood that the church would never
interfere with it unless they became a public embarrass-
ment. "After all," Ignacio had said once, "we're hardly
the only priests who are soul mates." Furthermore, since
the time they had started their ministries, there had never
been even a hint of disapproval. For his part, Lucas had
always tried to behave in a discreet manner. But the archbishop's words were a veiled accusation. He braced himself for an unpleasant interview and hoped that Ignacio
would keep his composure.

Archbishop Mota now turned to face Ignacio. "I
don't know if you're aware of the rumors that say you
have AIDS, Father Ignacio. I pray they're not true. As it
is, with all the bad publicity we've received recently, this
is one scandal the church would like to avoid."

Archbishop Mota was obviously referring to the stories of pedophilia that had surfaced in the media all over
the world in the prior decade. Ignacio grimaced; it was
a sore subject with him. He and Lucas had had many
heated discussions about how, in the public imagination,
homosexuals in the church were often lumped together
with pedophiles. Before they met with the archbishop,
Lucas had said to Ignacio, "Please try very hard to control your short fuse. Whatever happens, don't end up
speaking disrespectfully to the archbishop. I'm terrified
of his vindictive anger; I've heard of careers in the church
he has destroyed because someone crossed him."

Ignacio bit his lower lip and stared at the burgundy
carpet that covered the floor.

"I've consulted with other members of the Curia
about this matter," the archbishop said. "In the begin-

ning, I thought we could transfer you to a seminary to
be a teacher. But we've decided we cannot put you to
work mentoring seminarians, not only because you don't
look well, but also because of your notoriety. Damaging
gossip spreads quickly, like the flu. Apparently, you've
displeased important members of the military with your
careless statements in the press. So we think it would be
better if you leave Bogotá and return to the seminary in
Palos de la Quebrada."

Lucas flinched. Ignacio's face had become white, as if
the light of life had been extinguished in him.

"It's a place you know well, and where you could be
useful," Archbishop Mota continued. "In Bogotá, you're
a magnet for controversy that the church can't afford at
the moment."

As Ignacio remained silent, the archbishop turned
back to Lucas. "This is where you come in, Father. We
hope you can use your influence with your best friend
to persuade him that the Putumayo would be the ideal
solution to his difficult predicament."

"Don't answer that, Lucas," Ignacio barked. "I don't
plan to go to back to the Putumayo—now, or ever."

The archbishop stood up. "In that case, I must inform
you, Father Ignacio, that I see myself in the painful position of telling you that you will be transferred from your
church."

Ignacio got up too. "On what grounds, Your Grace?"

"Never mind that; there are plenty of reasons, believe
me. Don't think it has escaped our attention that your
name has been linked to several male prostitutes in the
gay bars in Chapinero, and that you've been seen doing
drugs with these criminals. It's my duty to inform you

that if you don't leave your parish in Soacha of your own accord, we'll have to remove you from the premises—by force, if necessary. Please leave your ministry with some dignity. You have thirty days to move out. Otherwise, you'll no longer be considered a priest of the church."

He looked at Lucas. "Good afternoon, Father. I pray you can make Father Ignacio understand that what we're doing is in his best interest—and the interest of the church." He stared in the direction of the door to indicate the interview was over.

Later, Ignacio said to Lucas, "Since I was a boy, I've always felt an anguish nothing could appease. But I haven't had any doubts about what I've done with my life. Over the years, I've noticed, my heart has turned to metal. I understand why God—if He exists—wouldn't listen to the prayers of a deadened heart. The truth is, I don't feel the spirit of love guiding me anymore. I shouldn't stay in the church, Lucas."

In the days that followed the interview with Archbishop Mota, it became obvious to Lucas that Ignacio had grown completely discouraged with his efforts to improve the living standards of the poorest in Soacha. He was crushed that he had lost the battle to gangs of drug dealers who were taking more and more control of the neighborhood. The gangs began to ask the store owners to pay for "vaccines" for their protection—just as the guerrillas and the paramilitaries in the countryside had done for years to anyone who owned cattle, or a productive plot of land, or a business. But now it was happening in front of Ignacio's eyes. Lucas saw him lose whatever restraint he had left.

One night on the phone, Ignacio told Lucas, "From now on, in my sermons during daily Mass, I'm going to denounce the gangs. I've asked my parishioners to give me the names of the people who are demanding payment for the vaccines."

"I don't think that's wise," Lucas responded. "You know what happens to people who stand in their way."

"I'm not afraid of anything anymore—I have nothing to lose. I will denounce them publicly. What's the worst they can do to me? Kill me?" Ignacio laughed.

Lucas had always loved his raucous laughter: when he laughed, he pointed his chin upward, and what came out of his throat was like a blast of pure air traveling toward the sky, like an antidote to the overcast, dreary days. But this time, Ignacio's laugh made Lucas shudder.

"I've wasted my life," Ignacio said.

"You're playing Russian roulette," Lucas told him. "If you fuck with those criminals they'll kill you. You're committing suicide."

"Listen to this," Ignacio said. "A man named Don Julio owns a shoe store; so he paid the vaccine because he figured it'd be easier than fighting the gangsters. Then a rival gang demanded a larger vaccine than the one he was already paying. Don Julio saw that between the two gangs he'd be squeezed dry and lose everything. The second gang told him that if he didn't pay up in twenty-four hours, they would kill one of his children. Don Julio took all the money he could from the bank, put his whole family on a bus, and sent them to stay with relatives on the Atlantic coast."

"Where's Don Julio now?" Lucas asked.

"He refused to close his business for good. So he went to the police station here in Soacha to denounce the extortion. Right away he realized the police were not going to do very much to help him. Don Julio received a call announcing that men were on their way to kill him. He didn't know where he could hide, so he ran to the church to ask for asylum. He's living with us now, Lucas. He's sleeping in the room that used to be Guillo's."

"My God, Ignacio, those men will kill you too."

"What else can I do, Lucas? Should I turn Don Julio over to them so they can kill him with impunity?"

Lucas closed his eyes and began to pray silently; he addressed his prayer to San Martín de Porres.

"Are you praying now? Thanks—a lot of good that's going to do me. Good night, Lucas."

"Don't answer the door tonight," Lucas pleaded. "Call the police and ask them to send some men . . ." He trailed off, realizing Ignacio had hung up. Lucas went to the chapel to pray; when he couldn't keep his eyes open any longer, he went to sleep.

It was six fifty a.m. when he woke up. Ignacio must have been getting ready to say early Mass. It was too early to call him, so he texted: *Are you okay?* There was no reply. Lucas decided that if he didn't hear from Ignacio by eight, he'd call him.

Lucas showered, shaved, and then went to the kitchen for his first cup of coffee of the day. He felt as if he were sleepwalking; nothing the people who worked in the rectory said registered with him. He headed to his office, drew open the curtains to let the morning light in, sat on his chair, plopped his legs on the desk, and stared out at the aquamarine sky. Now and then Lucas returned to reality when a plane flew overhead—like a migratory prehistoric bird. He remembered some lyrics by Julio Jaramillo that Ignacio loved, something about "the errant birds of memory." He was brought out of his daze when his phone rang: it was Ignacio.

"Are you okay?" Lucas asked.

"I'm alive, if that's what you mean."

Lucas smiled involuntarily. "I was about to call you. I've been so worried."

"I'm worried too," Ignacio said. "I found a letter under the front door of the parish this morning. It says: 'Mind your own business—or you'll be sorry.'"

"Don't go out today. I'll come by in the evening and stay over. Promise me you will stay inside all day."

"I'll see you later," Ignacio said.

That Friday evening, as Lucas walked from his parked car to the front door of Soacha's parish house, he saw written on the front wall with white paint and in large letters: "Faggot drug addict! Take your AIDS with you! Don't infect our children!"

Word had spread in the neighborhood that there were thugs who wanted to harm Ignacio, and the rectory was full of worried volunteers who gathered in small groups throughout the house, talking in hushed tones. Around seven p.m., Ignacio came out of his office, assembled everyone in the rectory's living room, thanked them for their concern, and told them that they should leave. To reassure them, he explained that a few people—Maritza, Don Julio, the cook, and Lucas—would be staying over. Some men offered to stand guard outside the house during the night. "No," Ignacio replied to this suggestion,

"I can't allow you to put your lives at risk. Besides, I can't be protected from those people every night."

When the house had emptied out, the cook announced that she was ready to serve dinner. The small group sat around the table for a hearty bowl of soup and a basket of still-warm bread. No wine was poured. The silence around the table was oppressive. Maritza informed Lucas and Don Julio that the two rooms for visitors were ready for them.

"Where will *you* sleep?" Lucas asked her. The cook, who was bringing the soup dishes to the kitchen, overheard him and said, "Maritza will sleep in my bedroom, Father Lucas. I have an extra cot that's ready for her."

Ignacio looked gray and distracted. He barely touched the food. The cook asked him if she could make him some scrambled eggs.

"No, thank you, Señora Tulia," he said. "I'm not hungry tonight."

Lucas was worried that Ignacio's fighting spirit had left him. He looked defeated. *Ready for death*, Lucas thought.

Maritza got up from the table. "I'm going to help Señora Tulia tidy up the kitchen. Then I'm going straight to bed. I need a good night's sleep."

After she left the room, Lucas asked Don Julio if he had heard from his family.

"That reminds me," Don Julio said, "I need to go to my room and call them. Good night, Father Lucas; good night, Father Ignacio. May God bless you for your generous hospitality."

Ignacio looked up and his face twitched as he tried to smile. "Good night," he said finally. "I'm told there's a new plasma TV set in your room. Sometimes there are good movies on Friday night. Try to get a good night's sleep."

"Well," Ignacio said when he and Lucas were alone in the dining room, "I think it's time for me to call it a day." As he tried to get up from his chair, he stumbled.

Lucas rushed to his side. "Here, let me help you."

Ignacio didn't protest. As Lucas placed his hand on Ignacio's waist, his hand brushed Ignacio's. His skin was very hot.

They walked slowly to the bedroom, in silence. Lucas helped Ignacio lie down, rested his head on a pillow, and then removed his shoes. Squeezing Ignacio's big toe gently, he said, "Footsie?" When they had first become lovers, if Ignacio complained that his feet were sore at the end of the day, Lucas would rub them. As the years went by and they stopped having sex, these shows of intimacy had ended too. But tonight Ignacio didn't rebuff him. His feet were clean, but Lucas noticed that his toenails had grown long and looked deformed. Lucas rinsed a towel in hot water and wrapped it around Ignacio's feet to soften the nails. With the little nail cutter he carried on his keychain, he gave Ignacio a pedicure. Then he toweled his friend's feet dry and dressed them in a pair of clean socks.

They hadn't said a word all this time, but once Lucas was done, Ignacio looked up and smiled. For an instant, happiness flashed over his face. Lucas went to the bathroom and got a bottle of rubbing alcohol to use on Ignacio's skin to bring down the fever. Lucas showed him the bottle. "I'm going to give you a back massage," he said. "You have a high fever."

Ignacio did not resist him. He looked as delighted as a child who has just been given a special treat.

Lucas helped him turn over and rubbed his back for a bit. There were so many dark moles on his skin that Lucas didn't remember noticing the last time he had seen Ignacio's bare back. The bones protruded so much that Lucas was afraid any pressure he put could be painful. When he finished gently rubbing Ignacio's back, he turned him over. Then Lucas began to massage his shoulder blades and his upper arms with the tips of his fingers. He became so absorbed in massaging Ignacio's skin, the skin that he had loved with passion when they were younger, that he was startled when he heard Ignacio starting to snore. Now Lucas could study Ignacio's chest without feeling self-conscious. It had been years since they had been so close physically, or made love, that the size of Ignacio's nipples amazed him: it was as if he were seeing them for the first time. His nipples were larger, fleshier, darker than he remembered, and they stood out in sharp contrast to the rest of Ignacio's emaciated body. Though not particularly attractive or shapely, his nipples demanded Lucas's full attention. He wanted to kiss them softly but held back. When he had finished massaging Ignacio's chest, Lucas took a cotton blanket from the wardrobe and spread it over Ignacio's body.

Lucas turned off the lamp. Then, instead of leaving the room, he lay down on the bed next to Ignacio. He had forgotten Ignacio's stentorious snoring, and he didn't have his earplugs with him. It had been a long, exhausting day. As he began to doze off, he remembered how when they first became lovers, he prayed that the two of them would grow old together. Tonight, it didn't seem like there was the slightest possibility of that happening. The last thing Lucas thought before he fell asleep was: *How will I go on without Ignacio?*

The first thing Lucas did when he woke up on Saturday morning was text Father Roberto, a recently ordained priest who had been sent by the archbishop's office to be trained in Kennedy. If things worked out, he was supposed to stay there permanently, because Lucas's duties had grown over the years and he had become overextended. "I'm in Soacha with Father Ignacio," he texted. "He's very ill. I'll be here for the weekend."

Lucas stayed with Ignacio all day Saturday. The cook, his secretary, the cleaning lady, and some volunteers came and went, hushed, teary-eyed, fear etched on their faces. Ignacio woke up without a fever but in a paranoid state: any little noise rattled him; if he didn't recognize someone immediately, he'd say, "He wants to harm me." However, with Lucas's help, he got dressed; then he announced he wanted to go to his office. Lucas tried to coax him to call the police again and ask for protection. Despite his weakness, Ignacio screamed at Lucas, "They're in cahoots with the military! Can't you see that?"

Lucas decided not to mention the subject again.

At lunchtime, Don Julio came out of his bedroom and joined them. He looked haggard, his eyes were bloodshot, and his hands shook so badly he kept spilling soup on the tablecloth. They all ate in silence. Ignacio barely tasted the food; then, abruptly, he got up from the table. "I'm going back to my office," he announced. "I don't want to be disturbed."

Feeling restless, Lucas headed to the garden in the

backyard and started weeding the flower beds, which looked neglected. It was a sunny day, and digging his fingers in the soil and pulling out the weeds had a tranquilizing effect. Now and then, for brief moments, Lucas could forget Ignacio's terrible predicament. Then all his strength seemed to leave him at once; he collapsed into a canvas chair he had pulled out of the shed, and sat still staring at the motionless blue sky. A wave of images from his childhood in Güicán began to wash over him: he saw himself on the farm playing hopscotch with his sisters in front of the house. Then he remembered the days when he had lived with Ema, while he was recovering from surgery. And he remembered—without pleasure, almost in slow motion, as if he were watching an aquarium—the neighbor with whom he'd had his first sexual experiences. Lucas shook his head to expel the remembrances of that sad time. Images flashed in his mind of the seminary in Facatativá, walking with Ignacio in the yard, so absorbed in their discussions that they could have been the only two people on earth. It was hard to control the rush of memories, and sometimes he struggled to slow them down. After he had been immersed in his reverie for a while, the green of the Putumayo bled into the present, and he could almost feel the stinging heat of the jungle. He saw himself with Ignacio going on their missionary trips to proselytize in Indian villages. In his dream state, he thought he heard the ominous gunshots that rang continuously in Palos de la Quebrada, mixed with the song of birds he could never see, and over the music and the gunshots he heard the haunting hollering of the monkeys. Then he saw Ignacio and himself entering Javeriana University, sitting next to each other in classes, spending weekends at his mother's house in Suba, making love all through the night, trying not to make any noise.

Lucas was immersed in these reminiscences when a chill ran the length of his body, forcing him to open his eyes and sit up. Suddenly he was gripped by a grim emptiness like he had never before experienced. He realized that after Ignacio died he would feel this void, this nothingness, forever.

The bells of the church were tolling six o'clock. Night had fallen. Lucas's face was burning from the long exposure to the sun. In the cloudless resplendent sky a pale full moon shone, like a disc made of the purest gold.

Lucas went inside the dark parish house. Without turning the lights on, he made his way to the living room, where Ignacio and Don Julio were sitting around a lamp on a small table. "I fell asleep outside," he said. "Good evening, Don Julio."

"We're having a chat," Ignacio said. He looked calm. "The cook will have dinner ready soon. Would you like a drink?"

Lucas sat down and noticed a bottle of Scotch and glasses on the table. He declined the drink; Ignacio looked like he'd already had a few too many.

At that moment, there was a loud thump on the front door. They all sat up straight. Another thump followed. The cook came in from the kitchen holding a large wooden spoon in her hands. "Father," she said, "I just looked out the window and saw some men standing in front of the parish."

Ignacio started to rise from his chair.

"Please Father, I beg you," she said, "don't go out."

"I can't stay here forever and hope they're going to

leave me alone. I have to face them." Suddenly Ignacio seemed energized, younger. He opened the front door before Lucas had a chance to stop him.

Lucas rushed to his side and followed him as he stepped outside. A group of young men carrying weapons stood huddled about twenty yards away from the house. Lucas could see they were on drugs, and angry.

Ignacio took a few steps in the direction of the gang, with Lucas close behind.

One of the men pointed a gun at Ignacio and shouted, "Just hand over Julio and you won't be harmed!"

"I can't do what you want," Ignacio said. "The church is a sanctuary."

A tall and jittery youth who appeared to be the leader shouted, "If you don't do as we say, we'll have to kill you!"

Ignacio continued walking toward them. Lucas stood frozen in his spot and began to silently recite the Lord's Prayer.

"Go ahead," Ignacio said loudly, showing no sign of fear. "You'll have to walk over my dead body to take Don Julio away."

Shots were fired into the sky, but Ignacio continued moving in the direction of the thugs. "You cowardly scum of the earth!" he burst out. "You'll burn in hell for all eternity! Go ahead—shoot me. You don't even have the balls to kill me; you know you'll be cursed forever."

Lucas closed his eyes. He didn't want to watch Ignacio get shot. *And if they shoot me too*, he thought, *I don't want their faces to be the last thing I see.*

The leader turned to his gang and said, "Let's go," which was met by grumblings of discontent. "But we'll come back for Julio soon. And the next time, if you stand in our way, Father Ignacio, you'd better be ready to die. There are many people who want you dead; your days are numbered."

Lucas opened his eyes. As the men walked away, one of them turned around and screamed, "Drug addict! Faggot! Pervert!"

Before they scrambled into their cars, they started to chant: "*The priest has AIDS! The priest has AIDS!*"

Later that night, when they were alone sitting next to each other on Ignacio's bed, Ignacio said, "Lucas, I've given some thought to this situation; I think the best solution is for me to kill myself."

Lucas had been wondering whether Ignacio was considering ending his life. He had always talked about suicide—if life became unbearable—as an honorable option. But on this night, those were the last words Lucas wanted to hear. "You don't have to die because you have AIDS. Too many people count on you." Yet even as he pleaded, Lucas knew his words were not enough to make Ignacio change his mind.

"It's because of them that I need to do this, Lucas. Their needs have to come before mine. My congregation doesn't need a feeble, bedridden priest who cannot attend to his duties. I didn't tell you, but you might as well know it now: the doctor told me last week that I waited too long to seek treatment, and though I can probably live many more years, it's just a matter of time before I lose my eyesight. What kind of life would that be? I wouldn't be of use to anyone then. I'd be a burden to you, to the people in Soacha, to all those who look up to me. Besides,

I'd rather die at my own hand than be sent back to the Putumayo." He grabbed Lucas by the wrist. "Just don't abandon me now; will you help me die with grace?"

Lucas said then what he hadn't dared to say ever to Ignacio: "You're what matters the most to me in life, Ignacio. Even my faith and my love of Jesus would not be enough to sustain me if you die and I'm left behind."

Ignacio smiled ruefully, lifted Lucas's hand, and kissed it. Lucas couldn't remember the last time Ignacio had been so gentle with him.

"I like what you've said. We're an old married couple who has seldom said, 'I love you,' to each other. Well, I'm going to say it now: I love you, Lucas. I know that without you by my side I wouldn't be able to face life for long." He was looking at Lucas with a tenderness Lucas had not seen in years. "Please, let's not get too emotional about all this. I'm perfectly aware of what I'm doing. If there's a God, I will be going to hell, right? But I'd rather burn in hell than continue to feel the pain I feel now. So promise me you will help me to die when the time comes. It'll be easier if you help me. Promise me, if you really love me."

Lucas's heart beat so fast that it frightened him, but he didn't want to make things harder for Ignacio. Lucas knew him well enough to accept Ignacio's words. He knew Ignacio would not change his mind. So he said, "Ignacio, I want to die with you. We've been together since we met in Colegio San José. I've shared my life with you; now please let me die with you."

"Don't do this to me," Ignacio said, getting angry. "You're not sick; there's no reason for you to die now." Then he exhaled and the anger seemed to leave him. "I do expect you to grieve for me, of course, but then I want you to get it over with and move on. Now promise me you will help me die. It'll be easier with your help. Please."

"I've shared my life with you, Ignacio," Lucas protested. "Let me share my death with you too."

"You're sentimental and selfish. Don't let me down when I need you most." Ignacio got under the blankets and turned his back to Lucas.

Don Julio managed to leave the rectory without being detected, surrounded by a group of volunteers. Two days later, Ignacio and Lucas got word that he'd made it to the Atlantic coast.

After their conversation about Ignacio's imminent death, Lucas noticed he began to talk about himself in the past tense, as if he were already dead. When Lucas remarked that he shouldn't talk about himself as if it were all over, Ignacio said, "Just because I'm still breathing and my heart continues to beat, it doesn't mean I'm alive."

Lucas began to spend every night in Soacha, sleeping in the same bed with Ignacio. Still, they weren't very physical with each other—except for an occasional, tentative hug. It was strange, Lucas thought, that after knowing each other's bodies for so long, they had grown shy of seeing each other in the nude. But Lucas's presence in Ignacio's bed seemed to calm him when he awoke from his nightmares.

For years, their long talks had been about current projects and plans to expand the social work their parishes were doing. Now they talked almost exclusively about the past, about things they didn't know about each other. One night when they had stayed up past midnight chatting, Lucas noticed that Ignacio was in a good mood and wanted to continue talking.

"You want to know what the happiest time in my life was?" Ignacio asked. He closed his eyes and then spoke softly: "I remember it so vividly now, like one of those Technicolor movies about the passion of Jesus that we used to watch around Easter . . . Remember them? Well, it was during our last year in the seminary in the Putumayo. You had gone for Easter vacation to visit your mother in Bogotá. For Holy Friday I asked Father Superior if I could stage Jesus' Stations of the Cross with the people of Palos. Father Superior thought it was a good way to teach people about the Scriptures—instead of giving them another long sermon. I organized a group of volunteers, and in two days we had everything we needed. I asked Señor Segismundo, the carpenter, I don't know if you remember him, to build a cross made of scraps of wood and to paint it brown. I wanted the pageant to look realistic: I filled up a dozen little balloons with corozo juice and hid them under Isaac Martínez's robe—I chose him to play Jesus because of his long hair and also because he was so handsome." Ignacio chuckled. "I instructed Isaac to stop every twenty steps or so and puncture one of the balloons with a pin needle I had wrapped with tape under his thumb. Whenever he pricked one of the balloons and the scarlet juice ran over his white robe and his body, the people watching the pageant would scream, as if they too were in pain. The people of Palos cried, moved by Jesus' sacrifice for us." He paused for a moment to catch his breath.

Lucas was shocked that there were still things that were so important to Ignacio that he had never told him about. All he could say was, "What a production that must've been. I wish I'd been there."

Ignacio made a brusque gesture of impatience. His eyes shone in the darkness of the room, as if he had a high fever. "Anyway, I had chosen to play one of the philistines in the crowd, so I could watch it all from the sidelines. I insulted Jesus Christ as He trod along the hot sand of Palos. You know, Lucas, that afternoon, during that procession, I found out something about myself that I didn't know before: I had created a spectacle that so transported the people of Palos they wept and threw themselves on the sand as Jesus of Nazareth went by . . . and at that moment I experienced the most perfect happiness I'd ever known. For the first time, I saw that my arrogant and prideful intellect had hardened my heart, and I felt the joy of having created something that moved people. I got away from that place in a hurry, and hid behind an old almond tree near the church. When I was satisfied that no one could see me, I wept, openly but with tears of joy, because my deadened heart had finally felt *something* deeply."

After he finished his story, Ignacio chose the date of his death. All that remained to be decided was how he was going to do it. "I can tell you what I've been thinking, but you must promise not to get upset." Lucas nodded. "I don't want to botch this suicide and make it worse for me and others."

Though it was a tough exercise in humility for Lucas, he listened without interrupting.

From that night on, Lucas too began to think of Ignacio as already dead. His heart filled with a sorrow that threatened to paralyze him. He envisioned what it would be like every morning for the rest of his life to wake up and not hear Ignacio's voice on the phone, or never watch a movie together in bed, or listen to his rants against the Colombian government, and the pain he experienced was so sharp, it was as if a knife were stabbing him over and over in the chest. For the first time in his life, he knew complete despair—which they had been taught was an offense to God. Agitated, filled with guilt, Lucas concluded that he had no choice but to commit suicide as well, after Ignacio died. In the eyes of the church, suicide was *the* unpardonable sin, and he knew that he would be condemned to burn in hell. It frightened him that over the years he'd witnessed how only those who believed in the afterlife seemed to accept death with serenity.

As the date Ignacio had chosen drew closer, Lucas's resolve was shaken, and he became afraid of the consequences of his decision. He had always been a timid man, averse to taking risks. He had gone through life trying not to make waves. Seeing his own cowardice exposed so nakedly appalled him. Lucas also felt sad about the things he would not ever learn now, the things he would have experienced had he grown older. He had always rejoiced in the unfolding of the tiny mysteries of life.

Lucas spent the last days of their lives at the rectory in Kennedy, though he no longer delivered the early-morning Mass. Every night he drove to Soacha to be with Ignacio. Daily, Ignacio received threatening e-mails foretelling his death. He showed Lucas a particularly explicit one that mentioned how he would be dismembered. Ignacio scoffed, "They better hurry up or they are going to be really pissed off when I get there before they do."

Lucas had always been troubled by his friend's nihilistic humor, but that day he couldn't help smiling when he realized that Ignacio's irreverent spirit—which was one of the things he loved most about him—was still fully intact.

A few days before Ignacio was to kill himself, as they were about to go to sleep, he said, "I know you, Lucas. I know that after I die, you will do yourself in—which I think is foolish of you. There's absolutely no reason for you not to go on. You're healthy, nobody is trying to kill you, and nobody is threatening you with expulsion from the church. But it's dawned on me that if you died before I did, I'd probably want to follow you. So I've made plans for the two of us to die together, if you decide that's what you want to do."

Lucas remained still, holding back his tears and his desire to embrace Ignacio—who he feared might be repelled by the show of affection.

Ignacio went on: "I learned of a young guy named Matias who will kill us for a fee. We're going to have a talk tomorrow."

"Don't tell me anything about him," Lucas said. "I don't want to know."

The next night Ignacio informed Lucas that Matias was ready. Ignacio had withdrawn ten thousand pesos from the bank. When he showed Lucas the bundle of money in a plastic bag, he said, "This is what he wants."

Lucas shuddered; there was no turning back now.

"Would you like to meet Matias?" Ignacio asked.

Lucas wondered if Matias was one of the hustlers who frequented the gay bars in Chapinero. Or was he a thug from the neighborhood? "No. I'd rather not," he said. "I just hope he's not a flake and he can execute the plan."

"Oh, don't worry about that." Ignacio grinned. "I've been reassured that his track record is impeccable."

Ignacio went to sleep around midnight, but Lucas remained wide awake. At sunrise, while Ignacio was still sleeping soundly, he got dressed and drove to Kennedy, where he worked for hours, writing lists of instructions for his successor in the parish. When he was done writing, he placed his house keys and folders containing information on bank records and bills to be paid on his desk. He decided against leaving a suicide note, as he thought it would be too complicated to explain the reasons for his decision.

In the afternoon he went to visit his mother's grave in a small cemetery in the outskirts of Suba. He placed two dozens white carnations against the tombstone, kneeled on the patch of grass by the grave, and asked Clemencia to forgive him. "I'm grateful you've been spared the pain and humiliation of seeing me die like this, Mami," he whispered. It saddened him that because he had chosen to end his life, there would be no happy reunion of their souls, as he had no doubt that his mother was in heaven and, if the church was right, he'd go straight to hell. He pressed his lips against the cold slab of marble, made the sign of the cross, and then got up and left.

Later, as he drove to Soacha, despite the crawling traffic, he felt at peace and grateful for the life he had lived. Perhaps he owed his optimistic nature to the fact that few bad things had ever happened to him, other than not seeing his sisters again after he had left the farm for good. He had tried to be a good priest: he had brought comfort to the sick whenever he could; he'd had the privilege of hearing confession, of becoming the recipient of his parishioners' most shameful secrets, of listening without being judgmental to the baring of their souls, of being present at the moment of absolution when their sins were washed away and they became as unpolluted as the day they were born. He had been taught to believe that at that moment God touched the sinner, because priests are vehicles one uses to get closer to God. He liked to believe that, as a priest, he had served as a conduit between God and His creatures. He considered himself blessed because all he had ever wanted was to be loved by Ignacio, and despite the many difficulties they had encountered, his love for Ignacio had never lessened, and it had always sustained him.

As the hour of his death grew closer, Lucas felt greater love for the priesthood than he'd ever felt before; the priesthood had led him to Ignacio, to being one of the lucky ones who had found a love that even death could not extinguish.

Ignacio went to sleep late that night, but Lucas remained awake, in a trance. He wasn't sure if God would forgive them for what they had chosen to do. *But if God is love*, he tried to reassure himself, *then He understands*.

Early in the morning Lucas saw that Ignacio was still sound asleep, so he stepped out of the bedroom and went to the garden at the back of the house. During the night, the full moon had traveled toward the cordilleras in the south; even at dawn, it shed so much light that it coated everything with a silvery sheen. Lucas recalled that January night, eleven years earlier, when he had spent his first night at Ignacio's parish in Los Altos de Cazucá. Now they had spent their last night on earth.

Eleven years later, it was again the month of January, the warmest month of the year in Bogotá, and Venus shone at its brightest over the savannah in the brisk, clear dawn. The morning star looked like a little full moon of burnished platinum; it seemed so close to the earth that Lucas wondered if it was in danger of plunging from the sky. A sudden chill made him shiver; he realized he was barefoot. Despite the cold air, and his freezing feet, he wanted to linger on that spot. The approaching sunrise made the mountains in the distance glow faintly like formations on a planet far, far away from earth. But this morning there was no time for losing himself in contemplation of the Andean daybreak; he had to hasten back to the house; he was ready for the last act of his life.

Lucas searched again for the morning star, for one last glimpse, but it had vanished from the blushing sky. His chin sank heavily to the base of his neck. He took a deep breath and turned around. Just before he went through the door, he felt a stab in his heart and his legs suddenly felt like heavy monoliths. *Ignacio's relatives will probably take his body back to their ancestral farm,* he thought, *while the church will bury me in Bogotá in unconsecrated ground. How cruel that in death we will not be together as we were in life.*

Lucas closed the door behind him and stumbled in the dark toward Ignacio's bed.

My Thanks

My friends Julián Mauricio Gómez Ocampo, Jimmy Luna, Alexander Aponte Moreno, and Alex Pereira played a crucial role with the research for this novel and I owe them the deepest gratitude. My thanks, too, to my agents Tom and Elaine Colchie for their wise advice and their constant encouragement, and for being my friends and family for over forty years; and to Taylor Larsen and Erin Clermont for judicious line-editing of parts of the novel and valuable suggestions.

I began to write *Like This Afternoon Forever* a few months after the death of my partner and best friend of thirty-three years, the painter Bill Sullivan. For the first two years after his death, most days I struggled mightily to write a single sentence; sometimes it felt like I was scratching out every word on the wall of my study with my fingernails. In that state, I wrote the first half of the novel. Then, in one of those mysterious turns of life, Isaías Fanlo appeared, and it is thanks to his loving support, his close reading of the work, his many important suggestions, and his belief in me, that I could finally complete this book.

And my thanks, also, to Kaylie Jones and Johnny Temple for embracing my novel warmly and giving it a home.